The Village
of
Little Figgy
on-the-Duff

OTHER BOOKS BY ALAN L. SIMONS

Eighteen Months- A Love Story Interrupted

The Village of Little Comely-on-the-Marsh

The Village of Little Pletzl-on-the-Zump

The Children of the Forest

The Incredible Adventures of Captain
MacDuddyfunk in Cuggermuggerland

Sweaty Cats and Baby Pigeons

The Village
of
Little Figgy
on-the-Duff

Alan L. Simons

BARONEL BOOKS
Toronto, Canada.

This edition is published by Baronel Books,
Toronto, Canada.

First Paperback Edition

Alan L. Simons asserts the moral right to be
identified as the author of this work.

This work is a fictional embellishment.

Library and Archives Canada Cataloguing in
Publication information is available upon request.

ISBN: 978-1-7782137-5-5

figgyontheduff@proton.me

DEDICATION

I thank my wonderful family and friends, who continue after all the years to have an inordinate amount of patience to put up with my unique sense of humour and style.

The Village of Little Figgy-on-the-Duff is the third and final book in the Village trilogy.

This hilarious and satirical story is about what happens to a distinct proud somewhat homogeneous community of Newfoundlanders and Labradorians, whose ancestors originally fled their homeland because of a fear the Vikings would make them wear traditional Norse clothing and take over the dry salt cod industry.

Now living for hundreds of years in a small village, somewhere in southern France, exclusively in their own world, without a care or a familiarity with their surroundings, they encounter, by chance, a 90-year-old stranger, an orthodox Jewish guru on his travels.

He's a biblical figure, who goes by the name of Gurdayal the Compassionate, a self-proclaimed spiritual vegan advisor and mentor to the youth.

ACKNOWLEDGMENTS

Once again, thank you "J" for your support and comments.

Shamelessly, I acknowledge I have attempted to render various common Newfoundlander and Labradorian expressions and terms into Francnewfunese.

To quote Voltaire, "Woe to the makers of literal translations, who by rendering every word weaken the meaning! It is indeed by so doing that we can say the letter kills and the spirit gives life."

To life!

My Story Begins

Let me begin right now by telling you about the village of Little Figgy-on-the-Duff located in southern France. It is a distinct proud, somewhat homogeneous community, of Newfoundlanders and Labradorians, whose ancestors originally fled their homeland because of a fear that Vikings would make them wear traditional Norse clothing and take over the dry salt cod industry.

Some years later, using The Rutter, the mariner's handbook of written sailing directions, they sailed in an easterly direction across the Atlantic seeking to harvest fish, birds, seals, and whatnot, in their small traditional wooden fishing boats that would have made European 15th-century explorers such as John Cabot, Jacques Cartier, and João Fernandes Lavrador, wet their breeches with laughter.

Finally, there they were, our fishermen with their kinfolk, one summer's morning they sailed into the Mediterranean and landed by chance on the sands in an area in France now known as the village of Salin-de-Giraud.

To those of you unfamiliar with the whereabouts of this village, I will tell you it is located 40 km west of the city of Arles in the Provence region in southern France. Arles, as I'm sure you know, is renowned for inspiring many of the paintings of Van Gogh.

While many of the group were basking in the sunshine for the first time, a few of them were exploring the area and realized the region contained a vast quantity of salt marshes.

Salt! White gold! They cried for joy, with tears running down their sea-faring weather-beaten Newfoundlander and Labradorian faces.

After much discussion, the group decided to split into two. The King, Mercer, Power, Smith, and Taylor families, who wanted to live out their lives along the gorgeous beach on the mouth of the Grand Rhône and exploit the salt economically, stayed, while the remainder, the Parsons, White, Walsh,

Murphy, and Brown families, who dreamed of returning to a land full of natural forest treasures, of unspoiled environment, of plateaus and cliffs had other things on their mind. Salt was not one of them.

With that, the dreamers said their goodbyes and sailed north up the Grand Rhône for 150 km, and for some unfathomable reason disembarked at Saint-Marcel-d'Ardêche. Thereafter, they headed east on foot for about 100 km settling in an area east of Col de la Maure and eventually establishing the village of Little Figgy-on-the-Duff.

What I will tell you about the location of Little Figgy-on-the-Duff is that it's somewhere southwest of Route D61 and the forests of Commune d'Establet and the Ruisseau d'Establet in the department of Drôme.

You won't discover Little Figgy-on-the-Duff located on any map.

Nor will you find specially-trained archivists, perhaps vacationing in the communes of La Motte-Chalançon or Luc-en-Diois, to be of any help. That's what its citizens wanted. Nothing more than to be left alone, in peace, and to continue speaking their unique dialect called Francnewfunese.

Dear reader, it is a dialect that for me is beyond comprehension. In that respect, I give you fair warning. I have attempted to render the vernacular into English.

However, in all fairness to you, a clue at this time to its salubrious location might be meaningful.

What I will say is the village of Little Figgy is not a figment of my imagination. The village is the final link of a scalene triangle consisting of two other villages namely, Little Comely-on-the-Marsh and Little Pletzl-on-the-Zump.

Quite recently I had the pleasure of visiting Little Figgy, albeit under the most unusual local conditions, as you will now find out. So, I shall begin the following tale by telling you an account of my fascinating journey.

The Village of Little Figgy-on-the-Duff

Lined with multi-coloured houses, the village is home to less than 1,949 people.

I ask you to first imagine a group of stores and whatnot surrounding Little Figgy's village pond, called not unsurprisingly, the Little Figgy Pond, a pond of extraordinary depth, of some 18-22 meters.

On the western exposure, commencing in a clockwise direction at seven o'clock exists the community co-op grocery store called Tea & Teeth, managed by twin brothers Rodney and Terry Parsons. Rodney is the older brother. On Monday and Wednesday afternoons, the store converts to a dentist and barbershop/hairdresser. Both brothers are well-equipped to handle all four vocations.

At eight o'clock stands White's Bakery which doubles up on Tuesday, Thursday, and Saturday as the village butcher shop. Jötunn White, a giant of a man, is a part-owner. His cousin Lisa White is his business partner. He's also the village's veterinary pathologist and primo uomo singer in the sea shanties and sailing songs category.

At nine o'clock is the Little Figgy Medical Centre and Surgery. Piddy Adfat MD runs the facility. Her husband, Baba Younus, is her assistant and receptionist. There are two nurses, identical twin sisters, Tryphena Brown and Tryphosa Brown. At the rear of the centre live a pride of Dr Adfat's famous Indian blue peacocks and their peahens.

Walking up the hill, continuing on the west side of the pond, at 10 o'clock, stands the only upscale restaurant in the village called Mudders, a one-star Michelin vegetarian/vegan establishment owned by Mrs. Violet White-Walsh. Yes, I repeat, a one-star Michelin restaurant.

It is here the Village Council, consisting of six members plus the Mayor, meets at 12:30 pm every other Monday for one and a half hours for lunch before their 30-minute council meeting.

As to their aptitude to govern, the Council's

Cabinet is known locally as the Triple F. The Little Figgy Flip-Floppers.

To the north of Mudders Restaurant, at eleven o'clock, stands the Little Figgy Cultural Centre. Margaret Murphy is the Executive Director. Every week four major events take place there. The Little Figgy Readers Circle, the Little Figgy Music Circle and Kitchen Dance Club, the Little Figgy Piddly Club, and on Sundays, at least up to recently, the Little Figgy Theatre.

The building also contains the village's Council Chambers.

On its right, due north, at noon, prominently positioned on a hill, is the Little Figgy Duff University, commonly referred to by its students as the DUFF, the acronym for Designated Ugly Fat Features, a name of unknown origin, but one illustrating its architectural monstrosity. Its principal is Jack Parsons, the husband of the Mayor.

To those of you who are members of the pursuit of higher education, research, and scholarship, let me immediately put your mind at rest. The DUFF is not a school of advanced learning in the truest sense of the term, at least not as you know it! It is simply a learning institution where the children of the village receive their formal education.

At one and a half o'clock is the DUFF Playing Field where Little Figgy's Piddly teams share their outside events with a host of spectators including such creatures as the European Rhinoceros Beetle, the Tarantula Wolf Spider, and the Yellow-tailed Scorpion. Wayne Brown-White is the Athletic Turf Manager. He's also the village's only Entomologist.

Continuing in a clockwise direction, now on the east side of the village pond, in all its divine glory, at two o'clock, stands the village church, the Gates of Heaven Help Us, commonly known as the GoHHU by its nine regular parishioners, where our Father John Murphy does his best to lead his flock in Sunday services. Above the church's entrance is an old plaque with the words, 'Quaerite primum regnum dei', (*See ye first the kingdom of God)*. Our Father lives intermittently in his rectory, ably attended, I might add for his domestic needs, by the widow Murphy, of no relation. His other regular abode is the Chummy's Pub.

At three o'clock stands the Jigs Diner, which serves home-style simple fare for breakfast and lunch. Chef Luke Brown is the owner. He is assisted, part-time, by his identical twin daughters Tryphosa and Tryphena, both of whom are also nurses at the Medical Centre. Chef Luke suffers from a complaint called Stereotyphobia.

Further south, at four o'clock, is the Little Figgy Constabulary, ably administered by Chief Constable Gabriel White. One immediately notices he has a medical condition known as Maschalephidrosis, a massive sweating of the armpits. He's assisted by his dog, Goobies.

At five o'clock, located nearest to the edge of the deepest section of the Little Figgy Pond, is Chummy's Pub. William Brown, a portly man, is the publican who has for many years been diagnosed with a disorder called Cenosillicaphobia. His daughter, Olivia, helps out the best she can.

Finally, at six o'clock is Burbots a fish and chip shop named after the farmed freshwater fish harvested in the Little Figgy Pond by Burbots' owners Zebedee and Karen Parsons.

And now today, this is where my tale really begins.

The Little Figgy Community

It all started one early morning, during the twelve days of Christmas while celebrating the centuries-old Christmas tradition of the Mummers Festival before the bells of the village church, the Gates of Heaven Help Us, rang out for the annual commemoration service of St. Fiacre, the patron saint for hemorrhoid sufferers.

There they all were at Jigs Diner, dressed up wearing costumes to hide their identity, as was the custom during Mummers. They were feasting on either of the two breakfast specials of the day, fish cakes, made with potatoes, burbot, onions, and herbs, served with baked beans or boiled eggs or toutons, doughy, fried bread dough balls served with molasses or berry jam, and as an alternative, the chef's steam-basted fried eggs, lightly sprinkled with cheese, are an indescribable addition to the toutons.

Both of these decidedly tasty meals are produced by Chef extraordinaire and owner Luke Brown. I have complimented Chef Brown for his creative ability, handed down from generation to generation.

Luke Brown – a man of respected girth and presence – was hard of hearing. He also was afflicted with Stereotyphobia, a complaint defined as suffering from monotonous repetition, caused by having to repeat too many of his toutons and fried egg orders to his servers.

Jigs Diner, for those of you who aren't conversant with the culinary ancient delights of Newfoundland and Labrador, is named after a hearty comfort meal called Jigs Dinner, which consists of potatoes, cabbage, turnips, carrots, and boiled salt beef. A meal having a unique cultural identity and I add with utterly no disrespect to its ownership, that today would make an ordinary sophisticated Frenchman and Frenchwoman with any sense of appréciation gastronomique française, want to... well, you get my gist!

But this wasn't France, at least not to the citizens of Little Figgy who continued after hundreds of years, to take their tradition very seriously. It had all to do with custom. Fish cakes, toutons, and Jigs Diner embraced a value they weren't prepared to give up.

Those present that eventful morning, amongst others, included Mayor Sadie Parsons and her husband Jack Parsons, and three of their four children, Jaxon, Jakson, and Jennifer; Chief Constable Gabriel White and his dog Goobies; publican William Brown and his lovely over-ripe daughter Olivia; our Father John Murphy; Junia, the widow Murphy, who is the church carillonneur and member of the Passalorynchite Christian sect, who years ago, much to the relief and wishes of her neighbours, had taken a vow of perpetual silence; Enosh White-Walsh, the village lawyer; and Dr Piddy Adfat and her husband Baba Younus.

If one wanted to show the utmost respect and benevolence toward the village population one would say, as I'm doing to you, they were quite an assorted group with medical disorders, including various phobia symptoms. And other than our Father Murphy, Dr Piddy Adfat and her husband Baba Younus, they all could proudly trace their Newfoundlander and Labradorian family roots from one of the Tickle villages, including Tickle Cove,

Black Tickle, Chimney Ticklers, Leading Tickles, and Tickle Harbour.

As to the doctor, Piddy Adfat, and Baba Younus, her husband? Out of deference, one never spoke about where they came from, other than to say the doctor was known amusingly by the villagers as Wad-a-Piddy! She had a habit of always shaking her head and raising her shoulders on hearing about an unfortunate event, while whispering to herself, "Wad-a-Piddy!"

Baba Younus to the villagers was commonly known as 'a pain in the ass', which admirably fitted his profession. Baba Younus was a proctologist by career, but he no longer practiced his occupation, preferring to just be his wife's medical assistant and receptionist. However, he had a calling that was appreciated by the village community. He proudly offered to volunteer as chair of the annual commemoration service of St. Fiacre, the patron saint for hemorrhoid sufferers.

And then there was our Father John Murphy, who, at this time in his life, had resigned himself to accepting most of his parishioners, other than Junia, the widow Murphy, had given up on religion. He was the only villager who could proudly trace his roots back to a small Newfoundland village called Dildo.

Jigs Diner had over time become a regular early Sunday breakfast meeting place for Little Figgy's young singles and mature bizarre characters all intent on finding a long-lasting relationship. And on this Sunday it was no different, except for an incident of which I will come to shortly.

The establishment is loud and brash, and service is non-existent. The tables are cleaned to the minimal requirement. The patrons believe Jigs Diner is their exclusive domain. They clash and ridicule each other, but just within the boundaries of respect. The patrons compete for love and attention. They might be different in age, but the language of love hasn't changed from generation to generation, just the style. The Figgy Style.

As to the mature characters, whom I'm more familiar with, they had been there, and done it, but not with much success. They're still trying to live in the world of their Figgy youth. They feel they are ridiculed and judged unfairly by Figgy's youth and therefore the village elders take every opportunity, through their deeds and jesting, to show they still have a standing in society.

In all honesty, the village cannot by any stretch of the imagination be described as being quintessential. Nor, on the opposite spectrum, could one call it wanting. Quirky or odd might be more appropriate, both in personality and in its population. I do not mean to imply I'm mocking its residents. God forbid! However, even though the village never wanted for anything and was self-sufficient in every manner, it suffered from a population bottleneck causing, if I can aptly put it to you, a genetic drift that was seeing a decrease in the size of the village's gene pool.

So, where am I heading with all of this? Well, I'll now tell you!

All of this concern came to a head during a heated discussion between Mayor Sadie Parsons and our Father Murphy, the likes of which were egged on by all those present. You see, Mayor Parsons, who is profoundly hearing impaired, regarded herself as not only loquacious but also as the leading bodhrán player in the village's Music Circle and Kitchen Dance Club. That was supposed to give her stature. In expressing herself as to why she had been appointed as Figgy's Mayor she proudly told anyone willing to listen that it was because the answer lay ahead in the well-known saying, 'She who knows the least talks most'.

What that has to do with her playing the bodhrán drum, I know not! On the other hand, her husband, Jack, an exceptionally gifted instrumentalist, was a fiddler. He also could persuade anyone with two left feet to step dance.

I will now return to set the scene on what happened during that early morning, on the twelfth day following Christmas, as the bells of the village church, Gates of Heaven Help Us rang out for the annual commemoration service of St. Fiacre, the patron saint for hemorrhoid sufferers. Now as a nonspiritual community it was the only time, other than for Junia, the widow Murphy, no more than nine villagers ever attended church services.

As the patrons were feasting on their breakfast, suddenly, the Jigs Diner's door opened with a bang, and in an episode taken right out of an epic religious drama, located in Roman-occupied Judea, a man of some senior years, came out of the shadows and appeared with blood streaming down his face above his right eye, and his hands bleeding profusely.

The stranger wore white clothing, comprising of upper and lower garments, with one open sandal, and on top of his man bun grey hair, a blue and white yarmulke adorned his head.

It was our Father Murphy, (who else in this dramatic scene,) on standing up, and with fear in his eyes, crossed himself and initiated the first contact with the stranger.

"Lord tundering Jaysus!"... thereafter, as his voice trailed off, the stranger fell with his face landing between our Father Murphy's plate of toutons and two fried eggs.

Dear reader, who is this stranger? Where did he come from? What brings him on this day, the twelfth day after Christmas, of all days, to Little Figgy, where in a few hours they are going to hold a memorial service for St. Fiacre, the patron saint for hemorrhoid sufferers?

Well, as my friends say in Little Figgy-on-the-Duff, "Wait a fair wind and you'll get one!"

The Stranger Arrives

THE next morning, surrounded by a crowd of Little Figgy folks, all looking at him in wonderment, the stranger, who has a multitude of polyonymous names in his own community, including the vegan guru Gurdayal the Compassionate, der andere rebbe, or just plain Yitzhak, as I will now call him for simplicity, awoke in Little Figgy's Medical Centre to find himself in a bed covered with a green, brown, white, and pale yellow blanket. His right eye was swathed in a bandage.

His bed faced an open window. The warm air flowing into his room contained the aroma of sweet thyme and overflowed with the scent of lavender, all of which reminded him of his home, Little Pletzl-on-the Zump.

In his younger days, Yitzhak was a student of philology and an avid reader of Ferdinand de Saussure, the founder of modern linguistics. But the folksy dialect spoken by those surrounding him had him baffled.

He therefore decided to follow the words of his guru, Paramahansa Yogananda; "Learn to be calm and you will always be happy," and not to open up to any conversation between himself and those present. He also remembered the Frantsoydish expression his Oma had told him, "Az men makht dos moyl nit oyf, flit keyn flig nit arayn" (*If you don't open your mouth, a fly won't get in!*)

The circumstances under which Yitzhak arrived in Little Figgy are shrouded in a cloud of memory loss. Sadly, and I say this with all sincerity, now at the age of 96 years young, Yitzhak always had difficulty remembering current events or freshly acquired information. Suffering from a condition called mild cognitive impairment (MCI), his long-term memory remained superbly undamaged, that is to the normal eye.

"Ah, he's awake!" Dr Piddy Adfat, the Little Figgy Medical Centre's chief medical officer remarked to all those surrounding her. "And now, look everyone, He's opening his left eye!"

Sadie Parsons stepped forward. "Who knit you? I'm Sadie Parsons and I be the Mayor of this place called Little Figgy-on-the-Duff." She turned around. "This here is me husband, Jack Parsons and three of me four children, Jaxen, Jakson, and Jennifer." Arm extended, she pointed to a teenager crouched down on the floor under the open window facing Yitzhak. "And over there," she said with a sigh, "is me other son, Jakob." All those present looked at Jakob as if to say, yes we know, he is a little different.

The Mayor continued. "Chief Constable Gabriel White and his police dog, Goobies." The chief, who suffered from excessive alcohol consumption and smoked like a tilt, uttered a grunt, his normal response to a situation with which he was unfamiliar. His dog said nothing.

"You've already met Dr Piddy Arafat and this be her husband Baba Younus." Baba Younus looked at Yitzhak with suspicion.

"And here our Medical Centre's two lovely nurses…" Mayor Parsons blushed with personal pride, "Tryphosa Brown and Tryphena Brown." The identical twins nodded, smiled, and half curtsied to Yitzhak's left eye.

Our Father John Murphy, of the Gates of Heaven

Help Us, hesitantly stepped forward as the stranger intently looked at him with his left eye. One could immediately notice our Father Murphy suffered from Maschalephidrosis, a massive sweating of the armpits.

"I'm our Father Murphy," he said crossing himself twice in the hope that his Lord would protect him from this stranger, while his left hand held on tightly to his rosary beads keeping track of prayers he was muttering to himself to St Dymphna, the patron saint of nervous disorders and anxiety.

A giant of a man stepped forward wearing a white apron with a mixture of flour and spots of blood on it. "This," said Mayor Parsons with a salutation of utter respect, "This is Jötunn White our baker, butcher, and veterinary pathologist. He's also our primo uomo singer in the sea shanties and sailing songs category."

All those present in the room nodded in agreement.

The giant smiled at Yitzhak, winked, approached him, and whispered the words that only Yitzhak heard. "But you can call me Joo for short!"

Few Little Figgy villagers present could have realized how difficult it must have been for Yitzhak, the stranger amongst them, the stranger who could only see out of his left eye, how problematic it must have been for him to keep a grip on himself. At 96 years young, Yitzhak, from the village of Little Pletzl-on-the-Zump, understood only one word expressed by those surrounding him, the word from the giant of a man, the word Jew! Of course, in his current medical condition, wrapped up in his warm blanket, he was not aware that Little Figgy's primo uomo singer suffered from a nasillate condition. Jötunn White spoke through his nose.

Mayor Sadie Parsons turned towards Jötunn. "Whaddya at? What's after happening now? Go on! Ask him where he comes from. And speak up. You know I have difficulty hearing you!"

With the satisfying thought and a smile, knowing that he had thought he heard the word 'Jew', Yitzhak whispered to Jötunn "Shalom," closed his left eye, and fell contentedly to sleep.

Jötunn stepped back and with an air of accomplishment having communicated with the first human being he had come across living out of Little Figgy said, "Shalom. He said Shalom. He comes from Shalom. Shalom."

All those present, except for our Father Murphy, whose face went white as a sheet, looked at each other and nodded in agreement as if they knew where the stranger had come from. They didn't!

Our Father Murphy, for the second time in less than 24 hours, crossed himself and muttered under his breath, "Lord Jaysus, he's returned, and to us at Little Figgy during a full moon on the twelfth day after Christmas and during our memorial service for St. Fiacre, the patron saint for hemorrhoid sufferers!" Our Father Murphy glanced around at all those present and then slowly at Yitzhak, the stranger now sleeping in front of him.

"Jumpin Jaysus. Why us? Why me?"

Dear reader, I write here of what I know. For no other souls present, would have known the depth of religious understanding our Father Murphy believed he had personally experienced at that moment.

The point is, I'm sure many of you from an early age have been brought up with interesting stories based on folklore and superstitious tales such as: 'It's very bad luck to cut your nails at night', or 'Women who eat goat's meat are likely to grow a beard', or 'One must not eat black chickpeas on Sundays.'

I can tell you for an honest fact, for our Father Murphy, the full moon has a special prominence in the category of folklore, superstition, spiritual guidance, and inner wisdom, the latter of which he believed he had lost years ago.

But, the arrival of this stranger from Shalom during a full moon, dressed in white clothing, with his hands covered in blood, and on top of his man bun grey hair, a blue and white yarmulke adorning his head, had a certain significance that behoves me to tell you the culmination of all these overwhelming events now on our Father Murphy's religious shoulders, had an immediate effect on his health.

Later that day, on visiting Dr Piddy Adfat, she diagnosed him as having saccadic nystagmus, of abnormal eye movement in his left eye brought on by a recent traumatic experience.

.

Yitzhak, the Stranger

I return to Dr. Piddy Adfat.

"Now, now! That's enough for the time being. Let the stranger rest. He's suffering from physical exhaustion amongst other things and is in no condition to be probed by any of you," said Dr. Piddy Adfat, usurping her professional authority. "So please leave now. Nurses Tryphosa and Tryphena will see you out."

At this point in my saga, before I continue, I shall do my best for you, for the sake of clarity, to tell you a little more about Yitzhak the stranger, since he plays a central part in this forthcoming melodrama.

For many of you who have read my previous Village story, *The Village of Little Pletzl-on-the-Zump*, you will have realized by now that Yitzhak did not come from a place called Shalom, but from the village of Little Pletzl-on-the-Zump.

Yitzhak, was an unusual character, even by Little Pletzl's standards. He was at the time a hard of hearing 90-ish year-old court jester figure, with one of the best Jewish law and jurisprudence minds in his village of 613 Jewish souls. He knew everything there was about Halakha, the laws derived from the written and Oral Torah.

He had a constant companion by the name of Shprintza, who in her youth was regarded as an accomplished four-key bassoonist. This bassoon is looked upon as the most difficult woodwind instrument to master since it demands all ten fingers to play.

Unfortunately, one evening some years ago, while cutting up some hard cheese for Yitzhak the knife slipped and she lost her left index finger to a very sharp knife. I ask you to give some serious thought to the situation, for it affected their relationship which, at the time, was also going through some difficult times. You see, how should I put it? Well, I wouldn't say Shprintza was an alcoholic but she had the reputation of finishing a large glass of the region's finest wine before you could say "Blessed is the Creator of the fruit of the vine."

After Yitzhak's relationship with Shprintza ended he became agitated and reckless, causing him to have fits of depression and memory loss, all of which led him to decide on a career change.

At the age of 92 years, Yitzhak entered a period of self-isolation resulting in him becoming a self-proclaimed orthodox Jewish guru, the traditional kind, wearing white clothing, comprising of upper and lower garments with open sandals. On top of his man bun grey hair, a white yarmulke adorned his head.

Based on his mission, he took a suitable name, Gurdayal the Compassionate, as a means of becoming the first spiritual vegan advisor and leader to the youth of Little Pletzl. His ultimate vision was to create a new vegan-based life for himself and the youth.

His idea was of course utterly noble and he gained a great following until he was found one Saturday morning to be eating honey. He was a mellivore! He enjoyed eating honey! Startled, his vegan youth minions rebelled and called him a fraud.

With his secret now discovered and with a lack

of support from his village friends, completely dispirited, he felt he had no option than to leave Little Pletzl and travel into the unknown for the second time in his life.

As he left Little Pletzl, walking slowly towards the forest, he stopped, turned, and looked back at all the curiosity seekers who had come to watch his parting. He gestured to them in a manner, not unlike in the olden days, when groups of wives waved goodbye to their Newfoundland fishermen husbands leaving for the Grand Banks. And with a flask of honey in his right hand he smiled and addressed them all:

"Effective immediately I, Yitzhak also known as der anderer rebbe, with one of best Jewish law and jurisprudence minds in Little Pletzl, who knows everything there is to know about Halakha, the laws derived from the written and Oral Torah, who entered a period of becoming an orthodox Jewish guru with the name of Gurdayal, the Compassionate the self-proclaimed spiritual vegan advisor and mentor to the youth of Little Pletzl, effective immediately abandons all that surrounds me.

"I intend to follow the travels of Gershon ben Eliezer ha-Levi and write an account of my journey, crossing the impossible Sambation River, beyond which, as it has been told, the Ten Lost Tribes of

Israel were banished by the Assyrian king Shalmaneser V."

And with those rather touching overemotional and historical words, he disappeared into the forest.

Sometime later, while walking amongst the bushes and twigs, he came across an oak tree where a short-toed treecreeper was perched. He gestured at the bird and said laughingly in Frantsoydish, "Nu! Az me ken nit me vil, muz men vellen vi me ken!" (*Come* on*! If you can't do what you like, you must like what you can do!*). Thereafter, as he turned to continue on his journey, he tripped and in falling his flask of honey hit him above his right eye with such force our voyager passed out.

Days later, disorientated, he appeared in front of our Father Murphy at Jigs Diner with blood streaming down his face above his right eye and his hands bleeding profusely. He was also short of one of his open sandals.

Dear reader, I pause so that you can compose yourself.

And now, if you are ready, I will continue.

I am sure you would like to learn that, over the next few days Yitzhak, as I recall, was visited by many of the village's curiosity seekers all wanting to have a peek at him. And just a peek it was. It was just the way Yitzhak wanted it, until that is, he felt confident in mastering enough of the folksy dialect spoken around him. After all, as a student of philology and knowledgeable in the field of linguistics in languages such as Frantsoydish, English, Yiddish, Hebrew, Punjabi, and Welsh, - hold that thought - he felt obliged to communicate with those around him.

That opportunity came the next morning. when Chef Luc Brown the owner of Jigs Diner, arrived at the Medical Centre with a big smile carrying a large platter of fish cakes, made with potatoes, burbot, onions, and herbs, served with baked beans, and as a special treat for Yitzhak, two hard-boiled eggs.

Yitzhak acknowledged his donor's platter and returned the smile, looking first at the plate of food and then at Chef Brown. He responded sarcastically in the only way he knew.

"Oi, a klog iz mir! Bist meshuggah? Az a yor ahf mir! A leben ahf dir. *(Oh, woe is me. Are you crazy? I should have such good luck! You should live. And be well.)*

Chef Brown completely misunderstood Yitzhak's response and he reacted in a hail-fellow-well-met manner with a joyous and exuberant laugh.

"This is it!" he said, pointing to the tray of food.

To which Yitzhak just nodded, smiled, raised his left eyebrow, turned his head, and fell back to sleep.

Dear reader, what you have just experienced is remarkable. It was, if I may be so proud to say, the first time in living memory that language communication barriers of more than one word were broken between Frantsoydish and Francnewfunese citizens.

It wasn't until the next day that Yitzhak realized what had happened.

"It is bashert," he told me. "Devine providence. Wherever this place is, HaShem is looking after me."

Indeed it was! During that very evening Yitzhak received a visit from Violet White-Walsh of Mudders Restaurant, the one-star Michelin vegetarian/vegan establishment. She presented Yitzhak with a meal that he alluded to would make him immediately offer his hand in marriage to her.

His dinner comprised of a salad containing grated beets, green apple, avocado, grated carrot, and hemp hearts. Followed by the main course, consisting of, broccoli, chickpeas, peppers, and carrots cooked in the famous Mudders cashew sauce, and garnished with apple, cranberry chutney, and cashews.

It was Violet who initiated the first magical words that brought the two in harmony. She looked directly into Yitzhak's left eye and said, "Eat! Enjoy!"

For Yitzhak, such words he understood and were overwhelming. A solitary tear slowly dropped down from his cheek and plopped itself between the avocado and hemp hearts. A message not overlooked by Violet.

He looked up at Violet and said, "As es kumt dein basherter, vest es visen in tsvai verter." *(When your desired spouse appears, you'll know it when you hear the first few spoken words.)*

He had fallen in love with Violet White-Walsh. For the second time in living memory, language barriers between Frantsoydish and Francnewfunese folks had been understood and had been reduced to paste, or I should say, to food from a Michelin restaurant.

The Case of the Easter Maundy Baked Mug Cakes: Part One

Whatever you may have heard about the origins of the iconic Mug Cakes, you should immediately put your mind to rest! I can honestly say, with the utmost authority, that they are all fables of numerous gastronomists brought on by their desire to show their Easter heritage of this tantalizing and scrumptious food, known for hundreds of years, as the stable comfort dessert.

Having said that, I can claim from talking with many of my Little Figgy acquaintances that it was Mrs Violet White-Walsh, the Michelin chef supreme of the Mudders Restaurant, who can attest to all that

I now will tell you.

For many generations ago, as the tale dictates, it was the wife of Captain William Whittle of Whittle's Bay, Newfoundland who left the secret ingredients to the residents of Whittle's Bay. When Captain Whittle died, his widow and her children returned to England. As a gesture of thanks and friendship to Mrs Whittle, the village community changed the name of the village to Whittles-less Bay. Eventually, it became known as Witless Bay.

Now, this is where it gets interesting: Mrs Violet White-Walsh from her earliest days dreamed of being a pâtissière. Mrs White-Walsh, or as she was known at the time by her maiden name, Violet White. She was a colourful person who separated from Will Walsh early in their marriage, just after their daughter Rosie was born. The details are immaterial to this tale.

Sadly, Will Walsh, or as he became known by his nickname, "Won't Walsh", died at the age of 23 during winter solstice from seasonal affective disorder, exactly on the day of his birthday, as he sat there in loneliness, blowing out his only birthday candle.

Violet, an assiduous character, with the help of her parents, brought up her daughter Rosie and opened up a small restaurant called Mudders.

Located on the sunny side of the Little Figgy Pond, between Dr Piddy Adfat's Medical Centre and The Little Figgy Community Centre, Mudders became an instant success, especially for its superb desserts, including the iconic Fygey Easter Maundy Thursday Baked Mug Cakes.

And here is where it gets interesting, so bear with me.

Over the centuries, to make things less complicated, the long original version of the name changed from Fygey Easter Maundy Thursday Baked Mug Cakes to first, Fygey being d

ropped and replaced by Little Figgy, denoting the local character of the dish. And, in time, Easter and Thursday were also dropped from the name, as well as the event you may know called the Washing of the Feet, or alternatively the Ordinance of Foot Washing or the Ordinance of Humility. And I can tell you, this was much to the wrath of our Father John Murphy, as he sat on his favorite bar stool at Chummy's Pub mulling over his beer.

All of this name-changing resulted, by secular consensus, in the name Mudders Maundy Baked Mug Cakes being agreed to, for, as it was said, it would be befitting and understandably less complicated to the charm of the village.

But I have somewhat digressed. I return to Violet White-Walsh.

Violet's insistence on calling herself a pâtissière affected her walk-in trade. None of her clients could correctly pronounce 'pâtissière.' So, eventually Violet resigned herself, with the greatest of effort, to simply calling herself a pastry chef.

And now dear reader, this is where we are, the Thursday morning before Good Friday.

Our Father Murphy, as was the Little Figgy custom, read out the traditional five-word Mudders Maundy Baked Mug Cakes short prayer to pastry chef Violet, as she commenced on her journey, much to the appreciation of all those present.

"Stir up, we beseech thee."

One could say, and I will, that the prayer was similar to a starting pistol used at sports events. It gave Violet White-Walsh carte blanche authority to start preparing her Mudders Baked Mug Cakes containing her celebrated and secret ingredient.

As she so articulately expressed quietly to me and in confidence, "Fruit. Yes, peach, blueberry, and apple are a must. So is honey, pumpkin, and strawberries, along with my secret ingredient."

She looked at me with a wicked grin. "I suppose

it wouldn't hurt to tell you, would it? For a wild and robust aroma I add some tuber melanosporum. You know them as black truffles. I picked them myself last night." She paused, took a long breath, and said with a straight face, "And I also complement it with lots of Little Figgy's 60% alcohol-proof brandy. It's aged at least 10 years in oak. Fit for the Lord this Easter, I say! Amen!"

She added, "It's indispensable, isn't it? Here, you must taste it, neat!"

Indeed! I relished the opportunity. I was not disappointed.

Perhaps it was just as well our Father Murphy wasn't in the vicinity. He was still struggling with Dr Piddy Adfat's diagnosis of him having a saccadic nystagmus condition.

Violet continued. "After it's cooked..." Violet White-Walsh pridefully pointed to a dark storage location at the back of her Mudders kitchen, where already hundreds of Mudders Maundy Baked Mug Cakes ordered for the eventual day sat quietly in their glory.

Dear reader, I am now preparing you for the worst.

To quote the great Chinese philosopher of

Confucianism, Xun Kuang, who has nothing personally to do with this story, he said: "Pride and excess bring disaster to man."

And so it also did for Chef Violet White-Walsh. Disaster struck the next morning, during the early hours of Good Friday, sometime before nautical twilight.

If I could raise some absurd humour at the incident, the proverb 'the early bird catches the worm,' comes to mind.

It was our Father John Murphy who first raised the alarm. On his Good Friday early morning stroll, past the Little Figgy Duff University and the Little Figgy Community Centre to Mudders Restaurant, he stopped and took a deep breath to smell the lavender, thyme, and rosemary. He also took the time to observe the prickly juniper and plethora of evergreen shrubs, as well as notice with curiosity, a muster of intoxicated peacocks and peahens staggering happily back to their pen as fast as their ugly legs could take them, with helpings of Mudders Maundy Baked Mug Cakes on their beaks and feathers!

Violet, who while arriving early to prepare her orders for delivery, let out a scream that was heard throughout the village.

Witnessing the scene of destruction with Violet,

our Father John Murphy could think of only one heart-wrenching thing to say to her as they both looked at the storage site consisting now only of small vestiges of baked Mug Cakes.

"Violet," he said with a sorrowful look on his face, "As it is written in John 6:12, Gather up the fragments that remain, that nothing be lost." Upon hearing those scriptural words, Violet let out a further piercing scream of such a high pitch, one of the sozzled peacocks walking in circles nearby, and smelling of Little Figgy's 60% alcohol-proof brandy, looked up at her, made a loud screech, rolled over, and fell dead!

It was Mayor Sadie Parsons, accompanied by Chief Constable Gabriel White and his dog, Goobies who were first to arrive at the scene of the catastrophe, followed by Dr Piddy Adfat and her husband Baba Younus.

On observing the scene in front of her, the doctor became utterly distraught. "What have you done to my precious Izan? He was the leader of his muster and my pride and joy. He loved his little peachicks!"

"Yes, he certainly loved his little peachicks. No doubt about it!" added Baba Younus, as all of those present encircled precious Izan.

"Your precious Izan? YOUR PRECIOUS IZAN?" (I add the capitals to emphasize Violet's tone of voice).

"What about all my Mudders Maundy Baked Mug Cakes? It's a disaster! All of them are eaten by your peacocks and peahens. ALL OF THEM! You're cracked!" To which Dr Piddy Adfat sarcastically replied, whispering in her fashionable way, "Yes, Wad-a-Piddy!"

"Yes, Wad-a-Piddy!" added Baba Younus, in support of his wife, as he looked behind him at the stranger approaching.

"Ay, what's after happening now?" It was Yitzhak, now fully conversant, well as much as he thought possible, with the local Francnewfunese vernacular.

Mayor Sadie Parsons replied. "Tis is it!" pointing down at precious Izan.

"Ows ee getting on?" replied Yitzhak.

"Wit difficulty! Ees dead!" responded the Mayor.

"Dead?" exclaimed Yitzhak.

"Yes, dead!" remarked our Father Murphy.

Dear reader. Much as I want to finish this story, I briefly pause to give you the full benefit of hearing the articulate, exhilarating dialogue now being spoken by all those present. In addition, I apologize for Mayor Parsons. She's somewhat deaf, and that's why those characters in this story occasionally have to raise their voices!

"Sometime overnight, he…" Violet pointed at Izan, "He brought all his peacocks and peahens up here." She gestured to the open door at the side of her Mudders Restaurant. "They went in, I don't know how, and they started to eat my Mudders Maundy Baked Mug Cakes, the ones ordered for Good Friday."

"And you," pointed Dr Piddy Adfat towards Violet White-Walsh, "You let them in. My gorgeous peacocks and peahens! My darling Izan."

"He's dead!" added Yitzhak.

"Yes, we know that!" butted in our Father Murphy.

For the life of me – forgive the pun – but as this drama unfolds, I am reminded of the renowned writer Edward Riche who authored the novel *Rare Birds*. You may know of him. There are some similarities.

Yitzhak turned to the doctor. "Are you going to

say a prayer for Izan?"

"A prayer?" replied the doctor. "A PRAYER? No, we shall have a full traditional funeral ceremony. The whole thing for my darling Izan!"

Our Father Murphy cautiously stepped forward as if to say something.

"Our Father Murphy, will you be the officiant?" asked the doctor.

I must say, I have no personal knowledge of a Roman Catholic priest officiating at the funeral of a peacock, and certainly, not a peacock who is the leader of his muster with the name of Izan.

However, our Father Murphy, being a trooper as he is, generously agreed to be the officiant.

Baba Younus spoke up. "We'll take Izan back now to our parlour and await further instructions from ..."

"Hold yahr harses right now!" Mayor Sophie Parsons stepped forward. "Tear be no peacock-picking-what-ever funeral service for Izan until we have a post-mortem. We have to determine the cause of death. I'll speak to Jötunn White, he's our butcher as well as our veterinary pathologist."

"How about death by stuffing himself while

eating my Mudders Maundy Baked Mug Cakes?" remarked Violet White-Walsh.

"Yes, that sounds reasonable," said Yitzhak, looking at Violet with a twinkle in his left eye.

"Now, now! Dis is nuting to do wit you! You're a stranger to deese parts," replied the Mayor.

Our Father Murphy immediately saw the opportunity to do what men of his stature do best. He intervened, crossed himself, and looking at them one by one quoted a passage from his bible. "Be at peace with each other. Mark 9:50."

.

The case of the Easter Maundy Baked Mug Cakes: Part Two

The next day, Mayor Sadie Parsons convened an emergency meeting of the Little Figgy Council's Cabinet to deal with the death of Izan, the peacock, and the appearance of the stranger Yitzhak.

Typically over Easter was the period for the villagers to spend time with their loved ones, but as Mayor Parsons told her husband, "I intend to work right through these issues so that we can immediately tackle this crisis head-on. These are two pressing matters that can't wait."

The emergency meeting was held in camera the following day, at one thirty. Those in attendance included Mayor Sadie Parsons; Deputy Mayor Lisa Walsh, and the executive committee. Allyship: Father Murphy; Health: Piddy Adfat MD; Agriculture, & Environment: Zebedee Parsons; Legal: Enosh White-Walsh, and Business Manager Annie White-Brown.

The meeting didn't start very well.

"Mayor Parsons." Enosh White-Walsh, in his capacity as 'Legal,' arose.

"I ask that Dr Adfat recuse herself from this meeting. If I may quote an old mid-century proverb by William Turner."

He turned to face Dr Adfat.

"By association and out of respect to you, I quote *Byrdes of on kynde and color flok and flye allwayes together*."

Dr Adfat, not known at any time for being at a loss for words, sat there in shock and I admit if I had any knowledge of medicine I would have to say her jaw muscles became so tight I wondered if she had acquired a condition called Trismus, muscle spasms in her temporomandibular joint.

Enosh White-Walsh didn't waste any further time. He continued.

"Mayor Parsons. I understand one of Dr Adfat's prized peacocks allegedly got loose and with the assistance of his muster, they entered, without permission, the premises known as Mudders Restaurant and took a fancy to Mrs White-Walsh's delicious Mudders Maundy Baked Mug Cakes. The Mug Cakes, I am led to believe, were awaiting delivery that morning, to numerous households in Little Figgy."

"And all paid for in advance," remarked Business Manager, Annie White-Brown.

"Thank you, Annie. Thank you for that important detail. Yes, all paid for in advance!" responded Enosh White-Walsh.

The Mayor raised her hand. "You have a point. I agree, we do have a competing interest here in front of us." The Mayor turned toward Dr Piddy Adfat.

"Dr Adfat, in a few minutes our veterinary pathologist, Jötunn White, will advise us on what his findings are from the post-mortem of Izan, the peacock, your peacock. Kindly recuse yourself."

At this point in my story, I have to explain my knowledge of local Little Figgy-on-the-Duff bylaws leaves much to be desired. However, I will say Dr Adfat, after much consternation and facial expressions, did recuse herself.

"Jötunn White, please advise us of your findings in this matter."

Jötunn White, Little Figgy's veterinarian pathologist, butcher on Tuesdays, Thursdays, and Saturdays, baker on Mondays, Wednesdays, and Fridays, and primo uomo singer in the sea shanties and sailing songs category, acknowledged all the village cabinet council members present by clearing his voice.

"Thank you, Mayor Parsons. Yes, my findings regarding the post-mortem of the peacock named Izan…"

Dear reader, I won't bore you with the finer professional details of the report, other than to say our veterinarian pathologist, butcher, and baker did an exceedingly dam fine job in identifying the subject's unusual details, contributing factors, what went wrong, and drawing up steps to preclude similar problems from happening again.

In essence: Izan was hungry. His pen gate was open. He went looking for food. He smelled a short distance away some interesting aromas. He went back to his pen and told his muster about it. They all went up in the direction of the smell, namely Mrs Violet White-Walsh's Mudders Restaurant. The side door had been left open. They were attracted to the odour emanating from the Mudders Maundy Baked

Mug Cakes including, and this is where it gets fascinating, Little Figgy's 60% alcohol-proof brandy aged at least 10 years in oak.

I continue. Izan, the leader of his muster and the most senior bird present, decided he had first rights to all that was in front of him. He gobbled down as many of the Mudders Maundy Baked Mug Cakes as possible. Too many it would seem. The alcohol content in them made him dizzy, resulting in him walking around in never-ending circles until his eating habit caused him to choke, causing him to drop down dead.

Jötunn White, veterinarian pathologist, butcher on Tuesdays, Thursdays, and Saturdays, baker on Mondays, Wednesdays, and Fridays, and primo uomo singer in the sea shanties and sailing songs category, concluded his report. I quote:

"Death by a loss of control due to a binge eating disorder, by eating unusually large amounts of food over a short period, together with the intake of 60% alcohol-proof brandy, resulting in Izan, Dr Piddy Adfat's prized peacock as "Death by Misadventure."

Mayor Parsons thanked Jötunn White, Little Figgy's veterinarian pathologist for his services.

Enosh White-Walsh echoed the mayor's comment with a "Wad-a-Piddy."

And on her return to the meeting upon hearing the outcome, Dr Piddy Adfat cried out "Fowl!"

And as for Yitzhak, as he later said in Fransoydish while joining his friend Jötunn White for a beer at Chummy's Pub. "De pave zol nit hobn di sheyne federn, volt zikh keyner a fir nit umgekukt!" *(If the peacock didn't have beautiful feathers, no one would pay any attention to it!)*

Little Figgy Council's Cabinet convenes

I shall now continue with the remainder of the emergency meeting of the Little Figgy Council's Cabinet convened to deal with the appearance of the stranger Yitzhak from Shalom.

If I may remind you, Yitzhak, since the short time he had arrived in Little Figgy had acquired a following that made a number of the community, shall we say, uneasy? It would seem, to some, that Yitzhak had overstayed his welcome.

It was left to Zebedee Parsons of Burbots Fish and Chip Shop to address the subject matter on the agenda.

"Mayor Parsons, our Little Figgy village has been isolated from the rest of the world for hundreds of years. Generations ago our people, Newfoundlanders and Labradoreans came here because we refused not to live under a social order alien to us. We found an autonomous land where we could be left alone to continue our traditions without interference. It has, I think we can all agree it has been a good existence. Our surroundings are clean and healthy. We are encircled by an impenetrable forest, at least we thought we were, containing thick vegetation that has acted as our security blanket, so to speak! We are self-sufficient in every way."

Zebedee Parsons of Burbots Fish and Chip Shop looked around him and stopped at our Father John Murphy.

"And then comes along this stranger, we believe from a place called Shalom. His mode of dress is problematic. His facial features and mannerisms are different from ours. He doesn't speak our language Francnewfunese with clarity, nor appreciate our sense of humor."

"Look around you, since his arrival our community has been swept away in internal conflict. And not only that, he is attempting to persuade our young people to become vegan. Vegan? My livelihood is threatened!"

All those present nodded in agreement, with full knowledge Zebedee Parsons did indeed rely on fish as his primary source of income, in addition to being a pescetarian.

"For his own sake and ours, he must leave as soon as possible."

Regrettably, it saddens me to declare to you the aforementioned details. After all, through generation upon generation, the people of Little Figgy had kept their sense of humour and satire. They were warm, friendly, and had the knack of being tellers of tales.

Mayor Parsons turned toward our Father Murphy. "Well our Father, do you have anything to say on the matter?"

Our Father Murphy arose slowly from his seat, without speaking. His face had turned beetroot red. He looked one–by-one at all those present and shook his head.

"Judas Priest! Hang on your draws! Are you all cracked?"

It was hard to remember the last time our Father Murphy had reached the potential of losing it!

He continued. "To quote a passage from Exodus: 'You shall not wrong nor oppress the stranger, for you were strangers in the Land of Egypt.

Exodus 22:22'"

Disappointing as it was for Zebedee Parsons, to my knowledge the matter was never spoken about again during Council's Cabinet meetings.

Burbots Fish and Chip Shop and How One Got Away

Zebedee and Karen Parsons, the owners of Little Figgy's Burbots Fish and Chip Shop, are Pythagorean pescatarians. They will tell you, without a blemish of shame, that they are the only known Pythagorean pescatarians in the village. I will not deny them that claim, nor dwell on it.

Zebedee's and Karen's family have the legal rights, dating back hundreds of years, to exclusively fish in the Little Figgy Pond for Burbot, also called freshwater cod. There are no known other fish in the Figgy Pond.

Dear reader, I remember quite clearly a quote I

once heard from an inebriated stranger while we both sipped our Moby Pale Ale sitting at the bar at a pub in Anglesea. The pub is called, "How One Got Away". As I'm sure you know, it's located on Wadawurring lands about 20 km from Torquay in Victoria, Australia.

The stranger, I will call him Jack, turned towards me and said, "Mate. All anglers are fishermen, but not all fishermen are anglers."

Jack continued to sip away at his Moby while waiting for a response from me. Little did he know I am not a fisher. But I tried to comfort him with a grunt, a nod of my head, and a shrug. To which he replied, "No worries, Mate. Fair dinkum! No worries!" Jack added, "I'm off to the loo!"

I never saw Jack again.

I repeated my story to Zebedee Parsons, while we drank our pint of Little Figgy Beer under the canopy of Chummy's pub, facing the Little Figgy Pond. He nodded in agreement and repeated Jack's comment with a sigh. "Yes, he's right you know. All anglers are fishermen, but not all fishermen are anglers." He emphasized the words *not all* quite clearly to me as if to tell me he was an angler.

Zebedee turned towards me. "Tell me. Do you think Yitzhak knows how to angle?"

Zebedee's question brought back to me the fascinating conversation I had with Jack and how I replied to him. With a grunt, a nod of my head, and a shrug. It had a similar effect. Zebedee put his beer down on the table, got up and went to the loo. But unlike Jack, he returned.

It goes without saying many people who ask questions are not necessarily looking for an answer, but instead, a compliment. In the case of Zebedee, he already knew from previous questioning I did not know Yitzhak's angling expertise. I, therefore, recognized there was a suspicious act in the works to which I was not priveé.

"Jesus!" I offered a response to Zebedee. He took the bait.

"Jaysus?" he replied.

"Yes, that's right! Jesus. Well, actually Revelation 7:13-17: 'Then one of the elders answered, saying to me: These who are clothed in the white robes, who are they, and where have they come from?'"

"Ah! I see what you're driving at!" Zebedee retorted with a chuckle. White robes and Yitzhak, eh! I get it!" He didn't!

"You know they bite best at night, after dark,"

Zebedee added boastfully. There was a pause between night and after dark while he looked at the last remnants of his pint of beer.

"Just over there, facing the Little Figgy Pond, that's where they are at night, in deep water." He pointed knowingly with the confidence of a proprietor of a fish and chip shop.

As Olivia, the publican's daughter passed us, he caught her eye and raised his right index finger in an anti-clockwise circular motion. A few moments later we had the ownership of another two pints of Little Figgy Beer.

"Yes, in deep water, at night. We need a few more anglers, at night, to help us bring in the extra fish."

He didn't wait for my "why?" before continuing.

"The annual Little Figgy Hootie Music Festival is planned next month, right over there, he pointed, at the edge of the Little Figgy Pond. And that's where we plan to have a special place cooking our renowned barbeque burbot dish."

The Little Figgy Music Ensemble

Tell me, what would a village be without a gathering of melophiles? Little Figgy, in that respect, is no different from other small communities. However, I admit, their taste might seem a little, shall we say unique, but generally speaking their adoration for music covers a whole eclectic selection of interests.

The Little Figgy Music Ensemble, commonly known locally as the Little Figgy Quintet, as I will now call them, consists of a group of five diehards who meet every Thursday evening, at seven and one half past the hour, at the Little Figgy Community Centre. Their music, for the most part, comprises of sea shanties and sailing songs from a long time ago.

Their musical director, composer, and arranger is hymnodist Delbert Brown. You may know of him. He is also chair of the Little Figgy Music Circle, famed for its hymn melodies. If there's one hymn that sticks in everyone's mind, I'm sure you are familiar with it, it is the rendering of the well-known version of, "It is not good for a man to be alone", arranged for music in the baroque style by Delbert Brown, with lyrics by our Father John Murphy.

It is told, in some quarters, of which at this time I cannot collaborate, that Delbert's ancestors were acquainted with the English composer Henry Purcell.

The quintet's musical instruments, as one would expect, include the bodhrán, the ugly stick, the accordion, and the fiddle. Mayor Sadie Parsons plays the bodhrán. Her husband, Jack Parsons, is the fiddler. Chief Constable Gabriel White plays the ugly stick, and the widow Murphy is on the accordion. Occasionally, if appropriate, the musical saw is introduced, also played remarkably well by the widow Murphy.

Mrs Blanche White is the quintet's lead singer. She has sung for most of her three score and fifteen years, habitually out of tune. But, she does have a lovely personality, as well as making a delicious partridgeberry cake.

It was the Thursday one month before the annual

Little Figgy Hootie Music Festival when all of the quintet's members were told in advance to arrive on time for their weekly rehearsal. Delbert had some news he wanted to share with the group.

"I'm excited to inform you this year we will be performing two new sailing songs at the Festival…" He paused to express the full effect of his next words. "Which I have written and set to music for you."

Mrs Blanche White let out a delightful timely scream, which in itself was unusual since she was always customarily late for rehearsals.

Delbert favourably acknowledged the scream with a nod of his head. He continued.

"The two compositions are called, 'I'm a son of a sea cook' and 'Love is sweet but it's tastier with a piece of fish.'"

"Blanche, will you favour us by singing Love is Sweet? And as a special honor Jötunn White, Little Figgy's baker, butcher, veterinary pathologist, and primo uomo singer in the sea shanties and sailing songs category, has agreed to join us to sing, 'I'm a son of a sea cook."

Without exception, all those present were in rapturous harmony, as I was, with the news.

"And now, here are the lead sheets for each of

you. Let's have a run-through, we only have a month to get into shape."

All the rehearsals, leading up to the annual Little Figgy Hootie Music Festival, were remarkably good, that is up to a point. I have no notion how it happened other than to say Mrs Blanche White, in one of her enthusiastic moments, presented each member of the quintet with their very own spicy partridgeberry cake. Perhaps it was the molasses or the pumpkin pie spice, or as Dr Piddy Adfat confided in me, perhaps it was the toothpicks inserted and accidentally left in the pie that most likely caused everyone to have a negative reaction to their digestive system.

Be as it may, I must say, all members of the quintet thankfully recovered sufficiently enough to proudly perform in the music festival.

And as for Mrs Blanche White? She admitted her rendering of 'Love is sweet but it's tastier with a piece of fish' bore no resemblance to her spicy partridgeberry cake.

The Little Figgy Hootie Music Festival and the Longhorn Beetle

If I had to suggest one important social activity that has the village in rapturous harmony, an event that stands out foremost in the lives of so many of its people, it is without any hesitation the Little Figgy Hootie Music Festival.

From its start many generations ago, the cultural impact it has had in shaping the Figgy people in terms of what and who they are today is immeasurable.

In your world, it would come close to being defined as being named an entertainment capital, an artistic centre of the world, containing the best in music composition, songwriting, singing, and dancing. One must add to all of these genres the playing of instruments such as the ugly stick, the bodhrán, and the musical saw, to name a few.

That being said, in the music field the village has its fair share of creative jealousy and that was clearly evident during a recent meeting between the chair of the Music Circle, Delbert Brown, and the chair of the Dance Club, Dalphina Walsh. Both chairs have a grandiose sense of importance, coupled with an obsession with their own accomplishments. Collectively they are known in Little Figgy as "Dee-Dah-Dum". I might add, that if they had possessed one minuscule spark of theatrical talent and been able to work together, I would have immediately signed them on the spot and booked them in as a vaudeville act at a major theatre.

I shall best describe the Dee-Dah-Dum vaudevillians this way:

Dee is short, bald, unappealing, poorly dressed, and corpulent. He features a unique moustache that you and I would compare to that of a moustached treeswit that is found in the habitats of, for example, New-Guinea and the Solomon Islands archipelagos. Dee is lisp-speaking, and short-sighted. His claim to fame is he has an impressive vocal range of six octaves.

Now, Dah, she never married. She's extremely thin, tall, standing head and shoulders above Dee, and attractive-looking with drooping eyes, a deep-voice with a high-pitched laugh. Her passionate musical talent is restricted to playing various instruments including a flute made from a hollow bird-bone, and the lithophone, both of which I'm sure you're familiar.

But, I'm sure you're asking yourself, other than their musical talent, what is it that actually brings these two vaudevillians together to form an act worthy of the stage? It is simply this, they are both proud unibrowers.

The meeting, as I will best describe to you, was to discuss the upcoming Little Figgy Hootie Music Festival, or as I will call it, the annual Little Figgy Hootie Music Festival, and how the Longhorn Beatle became part of the celebration.

For hundreds of years, the Little Figgy Hootie Music Festival has inspired the village's emerging artists, where they live and work peacefully in an inclusive, fair, and compassionate society.

The Festival has a long tradition. It was inspired by the original elders of the village to value nature and to preserve and celebrate the villagers' unique community spirit.

The Hootie team of volunteers is divided into two groups, none of them strangers to talent. They are enthusiastically led by the chair of the Music Circle, Delbert Brown, and the chair of the Dance Club, Dalphina Walsh. For years both have curated and organized a series of iconic and unique spectacles surrounding the Little Figgy Pond and now for the first time, a custom-made wooden stage located at the very edge of the pond facing Chummy's Pub, was approved by the Little Figgy Council's Cabinet.

Designed by the husband and wife team, Benjamin and Berthina Brown, professionally known throughout the village as 'The Coopers'. By trade, they made wooden barrels.

As pointed out to me by publican William Brown, "There's no one else in the village that knows more about bulge hoops, cants, or bottom heads than our Ben and Berthina." He added with a smile, "Take Berthina, she knows exactly how to head a barrel." He paused, trying to be kind. "But do either of them know how to design and put together a stage? I don't think so!"

Having said that, Little Figgy's stranger, you know him as Yitzhak, had been invited by Mayor Sadie Parsons to officially open the Festival, much to the irritation of Dah, of the famed Dee-Dah-Dum vaudeville act, and Zebedee Parsons.

Her vaudeville partner, Dee, was all in favour since he had put, as they say, a good word in for Yitzhak with the Mayor. And that is where the argument between Dee and Dah started, both trying to usurp their status.

As they say in Francnewfunese, it started as a maffle, then into a quaddle, and then into a full-blown battle royal with Dah calling Dee an embryonic bungfu squonk! Even if your Francnewfunese isn't up to scratch, I'm sure you get the gist of the seriousness of the situation.

My dear reader, for our two vaudevillians it didn't stop there and I speak here from what I observed. It was Dee, our corpulent entertainer, with a six-octave range and sprouting a moustache that compared favourably to a moustached treeswit of New Guinea, who resolved the emotional exchange.

I have no doubt the conclusion would have fitted into the first twenty-five seconds of the grand introduction of Carl Orff's Carmina Burana No 1 O Fortuna.

Dee walked over to where Dah kept her musical instruments and broke to smithereens her beloved flute made from a hollow bird-bone.

It was the end of the beginning of their vaudeville act and one that no longer encouraged me to consider booking an engagement for the two.

To return to the Little Figgy Hootie Music Festival.

Yitzhak graciously accepted the honour by Mayor Parsons of opening the Festival, and since the event coincided with both the first day of Baisakhi, the agricultural Sikh festival of happiness and prosperity, and the first day of Passover, he announced in front of a magnificent gathering of well-wishers he would attend as Gurdayal the Compassionate, the self-proclaimed orthodox vegan Jewish guru.

He told me, with explicit instructions not to tell anyone, that he would be wearing his traditional white clothing, comprising of upper and lower garments with open brown sandals. He added, "A white yarmulke will adorn my head on top of my man bun grey hair, thereby emphasizing the importance of consciously raising the need for social dialogue between cultures."

It was truly an admiring statement. Unfortunately, no one present understood a word!

The current year's event was undoubtedly the largest one-day festival held in Little Figgy. The event included traditional sea shanties and sailing songs, comedy, a youth stage performance, and delicious barbequed fish.

Was, I underlined this word and put it in italics to emphasize a theatrical mishap during the opening number. You see, the stage trap door collapsed, accompanied by parts of the stage floor and they all fell into the deepest part of the Little Figgy Pond, together with members of the choir, led by primo uomo Jötunn White, while they were all boisterously singing an a cappella rendering of the last two lines of the first chorus of Tickle Cove Pond.

Thankfully, all the members of the choir could swim as they, dripping wet, upon getting out of the water, and bravely still singing without missing a single musical note, hastily fled into Chummy's Pub for a pint.

Dear reader, it was not as fruitful for the European Longhorn beetle, or as you might know him as the hylotrupes bajulus, the primary initiator of the mishap. The species are not particularly known to be good swimmers, nor can they sing one single a cappella note. However, they are rather good at eating wood.

Jim the School Crossing Guard and stand-up comedian at Chummy's Pub on Friday and Saturday nights.

I have thoroughly investigated the whys and wherefores of the employment of a school crossing guard in Little Figgy and it would seem years ago, if I remember, – you can correct me if I am mistaken - the village's Council had a vision to establish a safety review committee to determine safety standards for students.

In due course they appointed a select committee, called Figgy Action Committee for a Children's Safe Environment (FACFACSE). The objective was to contribute, through discussion, to a healthy village by encouraging walking to school and ensuring walking routes are safe.

After months of deliberation and countless meetings, FACFACSE concluded their outcome would be pointless without retaining a school crossing guard.

If, dear reader, you have any reservations about what may be behind the FACFACSE conclusion, well, I have to tell you there's a story about to be told.

I am sure most of us, of a certain age, will remember our school crossing guards. Some of us may even remember their names. I do not! I do remember they looked ancient. They seemed to appear and disappear into oblivion during certain times of day, only to return the next school morning thirty minutes before school began and thirty minutes before school ended.

I share this fascinating moment in memorabilia with you as my method of introducing you to Little Figgy's only school crossing guard.

His name is Liol White-Walsh-Parsons. He's also a stand-up comedian. He goes by the stage name of "Jim" and that is what I will call him from now on. Indeed, you would be justified in questioning why the village needs a school crossing guard all decked out in uniform and a hand-held STOP sign.

I will tell you the fundamental trouble I have with all of this is the village is devoid of any motorized vehicles. There are no highways, arteries, main or public roads, streets, or the like, for children or adults to cross. The village's primary means of getting from A to B is by taking one of the handful of walking paths, none of which have been designated by any name.

Now, I will tell you there was a time, some years ago, that the Little Figgy Council Cabinet had arbitrarily voted, during one of their jolly Monday lunches and liquid refreshments at Mudders Restaurant, to seriously consider naming the Little Figgy walking paths and lanes with such names as Ticklemeallover, and DildoDrums, and Blowme-down, all I might add in remembrance and respect to the original inhabitants of the Little Figgy community dating back hundreds of years ago.

However, and this is where it gets intriguing. Such a suggestion got back to Figgy's chief medical officer, Dr Pidi Adfat, and her husband Baba Younus, who were most distress. They insisted there was also a value in remembering their distant past.

Well, Little Figgy's Cabinet Council discussed it at length at their next Monday lunch. Present were Mayor Sadie Parsons, Deputy Mayor Lisa Walsh, the

Executive Committee members led by our Father Murphy, Zebedee Parsons, Enosh Walsh-White, and Business Manager Annie White-Brown. Dr Piddy Adfat had sent her regrets. One of her beloved peacocks was suffering from an endoparasitic infection. All those present were deeply affected and sent their best wishes for a speedy recovery, to Dr Piddy.

However, as many of the council members had their annual medical check-ups coming up, they flipped-flopped on their previous decision and agreed unanimously to the doctor's request.

Unfortunately, as they found out after the good doctor had submitted her suggested names, they were either unpronounceable or the names were far too long.

I will continue.

The Little Figgy Cabinet Council, the Little Figgy Action Committee for a Children's Safe Environment (FACFACSE), Jim the Crossing Guard, and Little Figgy's chief medical officer, Dr Pidi Adfat and her husband Baba Younus, searched in vain for a compromise.

Indeed, the compromise, or I should say a

suggestion, came from Jim who was wearing a sleeveless yellow shirt, with the words 'I'm Jim the Crossing Guard' emblazoned on the back, who said, "Why not ask Yitzhak, the stranger amongst us, for his opinion?"

It was Enosh White-Walsh, the village's legal officer, who reacted. "Jim, get out of here you little sleeveen. I dies for you, but this ain't Friday night comedy hour at Chummy's!" The doctor and her husband Baba Younus gave their enthusiastic support to Enosh's comment.

Jim, being the artiste that he is, slowly stood up, raised his crossing guard STOP sign high above his head, and turned towards Mayor Sophie Parsons crying, "I resign! I resign!" And with a flurry of theatrical emotion, he started to sing "Remember Me" from Purcell's Dido's Lament, as he walked unhurriedly away from the Little Figgy Council Chambers, down the hill, accompanied by a pair of white wagtails intently listening to him, as their long white-sided tails moved up and down conjointly to the melody.

"Jaysus!" remarked Mayor Parsons. "I had no idea he could sing! That brought tears to me eyes!"

My story concludes.

En route home, Jim, now with an appetite from

his rendering of "Remember Me", stopped at Burbots Fish and Chip Shop where, with his STOP sign still in his hand, he ordered a special large portion of crispy potato fries, with the ends cut off, which he shared with his new-found friends, the white wagtails.

A short time later the Little Figgy Cabinet Council flipped-flopped and discharged the select committee called Figgy Action Committee for a Children's Safe Environment (FACFACSE) of its appointed task by rescinding the motion that originally established it.

Speaking to me about what happened, Mayor Sadie Parsons said she had discharged FACFACSE because of over-involvement by the committee and the change they wanted to initiate into the village's traditional way of life, and she was deeply saddened that Jim had refused to hand in his hand-held STOP sign, the only one in existence.

The Little Figgy Annual Piddly Sports Competition

If there is one sports event that receives much enthusiastic acclaim from the villagers of Little Figgy, it is the summer's solstices' annual Piddly Sports Competition, called by the acronym PIST.

PIST is held on the grounds of the Little Figgy DUFF Playing Field. To give credit where credit's due, the field is superbly maintained by Wayne Brown-White, the Athletic Turf Manager and Entomologist.

Much to our Father John Murphy's sheer delight and also to Junia, the widow Murphy, you dear reader might not be aware, this sports event, in the time-honoured tradition, is in celebration of England granting religious freedom to Roman Catholics in Newfoundland in 1794.

In addition, recently the event has added the name Tipply to Piddly, in tribute to our Father Murphy for his philanthropic services to Little Figgy, including his offering of a round of drinks, at twelve and a half o'clock, to all the patrons of Chummy's Pub, in honor of this celebratious occasion.

Outside of Chummy's Pub, on this day, at the deepest edge of the Figgy Pond, there's a large hand-written sign with a well-defined arrow pointed down wood. "No personal butt caps or handles allowed in the pub. Leave them here!" This term, I will tell you, is understood by all you anglers out there. For the rest of us, read on!

In Chummy's, much about the traditional game of Butt, which I will now tell you about, was being discussed by a group led by the villager's sports psychohistorian, Tanith Immilla Walsh.

As explained by Tanith Immilla Walsh, while her partner Wayne Brown-White looked on in admiration, the game of Butt hadn't changed over the ensuing years in Little Figgy's society's sports culture. Originally, eons of years ago, it was established by Little Figgy's avid fishermen, all over the age of 70 years, who needed something to keep them socially and cognitively engaged.

"Besides spending our time talking about the old times and drinking beer we need to create a game to challenge our physical and mental state," piped up one old-timer. "Perhaps a ball game based on fishing," another one added.

And that is how the game of Butt started.

Today, community sports games for mature singles are an integral part of life for many of Little Figgy's citizens and Butt fulfils their lonely life admirably.

Butt, or as it is called by anglers, "The Fisherman's Game," is a game requiring utter concentration, mental energy, and the ability to avoid accusatory words.

For those of you who aren't too familiar with playing Butt, I shall now attempt to introduce to you the basic rules of the game, which is played on a playing field of no definitive size.

The game is played between two teams of five players, each over the age of 70 years, on the DUFF Playing Field.

Simply put, to play Butt, the equipment one

needs includes, one butt cap attached to a handle, plus four butts, and one fisherman's bobber. One places the four butts upright in the ground, five cm apart, behind the hitter.

As tradition dictates, during the game both the hitter and the thrower wear the following outfits at all times. Fishing gloves, hip waders, and a sou'wester hat. One's color is of choice.

The game is played by a team player taking one turn each throwing the bobber in an attempt to knock down any or all of the four butts. If the hitter hits the bobber, the hitter gets one point. If the thrower catches the bobber hit by the hitter, his team gets five points and a pint of Little Figgy beer paid for by the opposing side. If the thrower knocks down any or all of the four butts by the hitter missing hitting the bobber, the hitter is out of the game.

Finally, and I say this with utmost seriousness. If by throwing the bobber the thrower hits the hitter either by accident or on purpose, Little Figgy's chief constable, Gabriel White, and his dog Goobies have to call in reinforcements to separate the two teams.

Yitzhak and the Dance Trapeze Artiste

Dear reader, at this point in my story I should apologize for not telling you more about what happened to Yitzhak, or as he's called in Little Figgy, Shalom, while he spent time, earlier in the year, in the Little Figgy Medical Centre.

To recap. He awoke in Little Figgy's Medical Centre to find himself in a bed covered with a green, brown, white, and pale yellow blanket. His right eye was swathed in a bandage. He was attended by the Medical Centre's identical twin nurses Tryphosa Brown and Tryphena Brown.

His bed faced an open window. The warm air flowing into his room contained the aroma of sweet thyme and overflowed with the scent of lavender, all of which reminded him of his home, the village of Little Pletzl-on-the Zump.

Facing him Jakob, a teenager, the youngest son of Mayor Sadie Parsons and her husband Jack Parsons, crouched down on the floor under the open window. The sight reminded Yitzhak he had experienced a similar incident in Little Pletzl's Zelda and Motti Medical Centre.

Jakob, now approaching his 18th birthday, felt secure sitting cross-legged facing Yitzhak. It was his regular place where he could withdraw from the world of his siblings and his parents unhindered by the daily squabbling and infighting between members of his family.

He knew from an early age he was different. He had overheard Dr Piddy Adfat explain to his parents he had a social anxiety disorder.

No doubt, some of this was fueled by the fact he was not only the youngest of his four siblings but there was an age difference of 23 years between his oldest brother and himself.

As Jakob became older he established a non-verbal means of communicating, mostly with a smile, a nod of his head, or a shrug of his shoulders. Conversation at home on topics such as who makes the best fried fish in the village, or the latest Friday night joke told by Jim the comedian at Chummy's Pub, didn't interest him. For Jakob, these subjects were irrelevant. For him, he was engrossed in attempting to understand the natural forest ecosystems surrounding Little Figgy, the scientific study of trees and more importantly, now with the visit of the stranger facing him in the Medical Centre's bed, what lay beyond Little Figgy's environs.

To return to Yitzhak. He quite enjoyed the extraordinary attention he was receiving from his hosts. They were quite a nice bunch of people and certainly, they couldn't do enough for this stranger, who now, with a strong Frantsoydisher accent, had learned to chat to his hosts, much to the curiosity of Jakob.

Yitzhak, for his remarkable return to some normality, gave much credit to his two nurses, Tryphosa and Tryphena Brown. On the other hand, as far as the doctor, Dr Piddy Adfat, well, that was something else. And her husband Baba Younus? As Yitzhak confided to me, "Oy vey! It is a disgrace for a man to be his wife's wife."

But if Yitzhak had one favourite amongst all the Little Figgy community it was, without doubt, Violet White-Walsh. Over the ensuing days at the medical centre, he had become fascinated by her exceptional talent of cooking vegan-based meals for him. And now, since the bandage had been taken off of his right eye, his ability to see had plainly given him the right to also acknowledge her looks.

Yitzhak took all the comings and goings in his stride. His decision at the beginning of his adventure of not uttering a single word to his hosts had reaped enormous benefits for him.

Yet, now such a mirage of deception was becoming more and more difficult. He felt caged in bed and his smiles, together with the twinkle in both of his eyes to all the visitors surrounding him, were becoming more challenging to produce.

All of this was broken one lunchtime by the arrival of Dr Piddy Adfat, followed behind her by Baba Younus. She immediately, as one would expect, took control of the situation.

"This is a medical centre not," she looked directly at Yitzhak, "not a celebration of a virgin birth. Please, all of you, leave the premises right now and, if you need to, go and make an appointment with our Father Murphy."

In a wink of an eye, or in Yitzhak's case, two eyes, other than for the identical twin nurses Tryphosa and Tryphena Brown, the Little Figgy

Medical Centre became a deserted wilderness.

All of this was observed by Jakob, who sat there crossed-legged under the open window, facing Yitzhak.

Nurse Tryphosa was immensely proud of her profession. She took her duties with the utmost concern fulfilling the needs expected of her, and ensuring the Medical Centre's only patient, the stranger Yitzhak, received the uppermost care. She had taken the role of being the primary care nurse on the basis she had been born a few minutes before Tryphena, her sister.

In that respect, she initially attempted to verbally communicate with Yitzhak and when that originally didn't work she did her darndest to expand into sign language, and then into manually coded language. Nothing worked! As she said to her sister, "He looks with his eyes, listens with his ears, and understands like a wall!" Little did she know!

Her sister Nurse Tryphena, was somewhat of a different character. She had other goals, other than nursing. And what goals they were! Two in particular stood out. She wanted to pursue a career either as a pirouette dancer or as a dance trapeze artiste. After much deliberation, she chose to be a dance trapeze artiste.

Now, as you're quite aware, the place I come from is somewhat different from that of the Little Figgys of this world, so I was quite fascinated to know how Nurse Tryphena intended to proceed with her passion.

But, before I go into that, I must explain. Nurse Tryphena suffers from mild body dysmorphia disorder, BDD. The condition, so I understand, can seriously affect one's daily life. Her twin sister Tryphona, to my knowledge, is clear of this condition.

The circumstances of how Tryphena attained BDD are left to one's imagination. It is an imagination that I am not privy to. However, I will say this, Tryphena devotes an inordinate time to combing her hair and comparing her looks with other women, and she seems to have an adverse reaction to looking at herself in a mirror.

As I'm sure, many of you are aware, a dance trapeze artiste must maintain a resemblance of being physically fit and must be dedicated to training and taking care of one's body to sustain peak performance, and also accept a high level of pain tolerance.

It is in this demand I personally had doubts about

Nurse Tryphena's ability to rise up to the challenge.

Fortunately, it was one of the twin brothers of the Little Figgy Tea & Teeth Community Co-op Grocery Store, Rodney Parsons, the store that converts every Monday and Wednesday to a dentist and barbershop /hairdresser, who not only saw the benefits of helping out Tryphena's dream come true, but felt it was also good for business.

And that, dear reader, came about on Wednesday afternoon, in the medical centres' tranquillity room, while Rodney Parsons was giving Yitzhak a shampoo and trim.

Rodney gestured to Yitzhak and pointed to Nurse Tryphena while gently trimming Yitzhak's man bun. "You know, she really wants to be a dance trapeze artiste."

Well, as I have mentioned, if I had any doubts about Nurse Tryphena's ability, it was Yitzhak who immediately saw an opportunity. An opportunity that to me had ridiculous overtones. But, as they say, it is what it is!

I hesitate to say this, but in any community, in any village, town, or city, one is going to find terrible teasers. It would seem Yitzhak, at this particular juncture in his life, resembles this character admirably.

"Rodney, she's such a beautiful girl for you, even though she…" Yitzhak looked directly at Nurse Tryphena. "… She does have certain, how can I put it, imperfections?"

Rodney didn't miss a beat. He continued trimming Yitzhak's man bun as he glanced at Nurse Tryphena while she ate her vegan lunch sandwich prepared by none other than Violet White-Walsh herself, consisting of green apple, grated carrot, grated beets with a basil, garlic, and lemon juice mayonnaise sauce.

"Well at least for a future dance trapeze artiste, she certainly knows the right food to eat," piped in Yitzhak. "You have to give her credit for that!"

"I think I can help her. My brother Terry and I have a storage shed at the back of our shop containing some of the equipment she will need," said Rodney as he completed Yitzhak's trimming.

And that's how it all started. Rodney and Nurse Tryphena started to work together. First on the preliminary training required, including cardio exercises to get the blood flowing, comprising of running, squat jumping, and power walking. All of this was followed by a routine of stretching to prevent injury.

Yes, indeed, I repeat, and that's how it all

started, that is, until Nurse Tryphena discovered, through talking to Dr Piddy Adfat, that if she had to spend an inordinate amount of time hanging upside down, it could result in an increase in blood pressure to her eyes that may damage them.

However, there is a happy ending to this fascinating story. Rodney became so besotted with Nurse Tryphena, that he asked her to marry him.

Fast forward. At the wedding ceremony, officiated by our Father Murphy, our Yitzhak was asked by the bride and groom to make a toast.

"Vu liebshaft, dort iz klein engshaft." *(Where there is love, it never feels crowded),* he said in Fransoydish.

The toast was welcomed by all those present, except Dr Piddy Adfat, her husband Baba Younis, the lawyer Enosh White-Walsh, and Zebedee Parsons the Pythagorean pescetarian from the Burbots Fish and Chip Shop.

Jakob and the Portrait of a Girl

Meanwhile, I will now return to tell you what was happening back at the Little Figgy Medical Centre. The main characters in this narrative include Mayor Sadie Parsons and Jack Parsons, the principal of Little Figgy DUFF University, Jakob, their youngest son, Dr Piddy Adfat, and our own Yitzhak.

It would seem Dr Piddy Adfat had discharged Yitzhak from the facility, but in a fit of kindness unheard of by many of Little Figgy's folks that I spoke to, without any reason she had allowed Yitzhak, temporarily mind you, to use the Tranquillity Room as his primary dwelling location.

At the same time, Jakob presented himself to

Yitzhak by silently following him to the Tranquillity Room where he plonked himself down, yes, under the window, crossed his legs, folded his arms, and stared intently at the art located behind Yitzhak's steel-framed camp bed.

Called, I believe, *Portrait of a Girl*, allegedly by Sir Peter Paul Rubens, the painting is utterly unimportant to this story, except that is, I presume to a forensic art conservator. I will therefore talk no further about it.

However, in passing, under the circumstances, I have to add a few words. Yitzhak was fascinated by Jakob's preoccupation with the painting. Jakob could not take his eyes off of it.

This was shared by Jakob's parents who were at the medical centre to attend a meeting about their son with Dr Piddy Adfat

"Perhaps it's a stage in his life. I wish he had some friends. Doctor would do you think?" asked Mayor Sadie Parsons.

"You know, Jakob's been this way since he was a young boy. He's always been shy," added Jack Parsons.

"Mayor Parsons glanced over her shoulder towards where her son sat absorbed looking at the painting while Yitzhak lay on his bed out of view.

"Mayor Parsons. Mr Parsons. This is not the first time I have discussed Jakob with you. My opinion is he's suffering from a mental condition called Social Anxiety Disorder, SAD. He has a fear of being judged by others, meeting new people, and going to a social gathering." The doctor paused.

"However, it is a condition that can, normally, in my opinion, be reversed. He needs to seek help from a therapist and I know the very person who can help him."

It was at this meeting that the therapist the doctor had recommended was none other than Junia, the widow Murphy, the Gates of Heaven Help Us church carillonneur and member of the Passalorynchite Christian sect, who had taken a vow of perpetual silence.

"Maybe we should consider getting a second opinion," Mayor Parsons said to her husband as they walked home.

"A second opinion? With whom? Have you forgotten Adfat is the only medical doctor we have in the village that is other than her retired proctologist husband Baba Younis"

"Yes, I'm aware! But you do know what I mean. Adfat, well, she's really not one of us, is she? I'm sure that after all the years she has lived in Little Figgy she hasn't even begun to understand our customs and culture. Maybe we should consult our Father Murphy."

"What! That pathetic individual who spends most of his time drinking at Chummy's Pub? No son of mine is going to be . . . ."

With these final words, the two of them found silent agreement in emotionally preparing themselves for the Thursday evening's weekly Figgy musical quintet rehearsal, held at the Little Figgy Community Centre. One a bodhrán player, the other a fiddler.

Dear reader, after overhearing the conversation between the doctor and Jakob's parents, and fueled by his empathy and curiosity towards Jakob, Yitzhak set himself the task of befriending Jakob. As he reminded himself, he had witnessed a similar incident with a teenager in his village of Little Pletzl-on-the-Zump.

And so it came to pass, Yitzhak took Jakob under his wing. While Jakob listened, Yitzhak told him a story about a timid lonely boy called Twm who grew up in the village of Little Comely-on-the-Marsh, located just several hours walk from Little Figgy. Twm enjoyed the outdoors, fishing and often he would walk around Little Comely's village pond, gazing at the water, wondering if he would soon be able to catch a farmed rainbow trout.

Within a short time, the language barrier between Yitzhak and Jakob disappeared and for the first time, Jakob found a real friend in Yitzhak, albeit some 74 years older than he was.

For Yitzhak, all the fresh air, the familiar pond, the village residents, and the environment surrounding him in this place called Little Figgy-on-the-Duff brought back memories of both Little Comely-on-the-Marsh and Little Pletzl-on-the-Zump. He shared all his memories with Jakob including the honest fact that his name wasn't Shalom, as he was called by mistake by the Little Figgy residents, but his name was Yitzhak, meaning one who laughs or rejoices, in the Hebrew language.

"Jakob, it's time for you to laugh again. Let's work on it, you, me, and yes, the widow Murphy. Together!"

For the first time in many years, Jakob spoke. "Yes, with your help, I am willing to try!"

Dear reader. How extraordinary life can be!

Here we have Yitzhak, a stranger with a profoundly different culture and tradition, befriended by a community of Newfoundlander and Labradorians living for hundreds of years in isolation in southern France, who speak a dialect called Francnewfunese, whose very nature makes him feel as much as home here as anyone could avail themselves of.

And Yitzhak, strange as it might be to some, with no ultra-motives, other than to anxiously show compassion towards Jakob in helping him return to some normalcy within his family and society.

But, I wonder, is that odd? Well, I want to remind you of Yitzhak's background.

He had lived in the villages of Little Comely-on-the-Marsh, an eccentric Welsh community with 347 inhabitants, and Little Pletzl-on-the-Zump, a community of 613 Yiddish-speaking residents, both of these villages of which I have attested to in previous stories.

Little Comely and Little Pletzl were something from another era, living up to the expectations, traditions, and rituals that no longer existed in their citizen's home countries. Both villages were self-sufficient in every aspect, never needing to introduce anything French into their villages. No French veggies, fruit, or meat for them, and indeed no French wine, and certainly I will emphasize no potatoes! Both village communities know who precisely they are, and strange as it might seem, it remains a mystery that both villages, even though they are but a short distance from each other, do not know of each other's existence.

And along comes Yitzhak, formerly known in Little Comely as Captain Idris, the village's 89-year-old legal representative who knew everything there was to know about 12th-century Welsh law called *Cyfraith Hywel*, but little else. Captain Idris, who self-appointed himself in the uniform of a WWI Royal Flying Corps pilot, who decked himself out with a leather hat and goggles, the traditional white silk scarf and leather jacket, who had a companion named Aelwen, a life-size blow-up doll, dressed to kill and always attached to the Captain's left foot.

And two years later in the village of Little Pletzl Captain Idris, strangely is identified as Yitzhak, a very deaf 91-year-old court jester figure, with one of the best Jewish law and jurisprudence minds in the village who knows everything there was to know about Halakha, the laws derived from the written and Oral Torah, who was called der andere rebbe *(the other rabbi)*, who at the age of 92 years entered a period of self-isolation, which resulted in him becoming a self-proclaimed orthodox Jewish guru with the name of Gurdayal the Compassionate, who had a companion named Shprintza, once regarded as an accomplished four-key bassoonist, known as the most difficult woodwind instrument to master, who regrettably, while cutting up some hard cheese, she lost her left index finger to a very sharp kitchen knife.

And now, my dear reader, Yitzhak strangely emerges in Little Figgy.

If I may be allowed to share something else with you.

If there's one recurring theme in this chapter and generally the rule in my life, living as I have in southern France for many years, and meeting the characters in the villages of Little Comely, Little Pletzl, and Little Figgy, it is that anytime one thinks one really knows something, one is going to find out one is wrong.

This is particularly true at present regarding Junia, the widow Murphy, our Gates of Heaven Help Us church carillonneur and member of the Passalorynchite Christian sect, who, had taken a vow of perpetual silence.

You see, what assumptions you might have gathered so far about Junia will, as I found out, be completely incorrect. For, I will reveal to you Junia, the widow Murphy, in the traditional biblical sense, is a modern-day apostle elder in the apostolic movement. She is hospitable, self-controlled, and holy.

And now, to return to Yitzhak, again. At the age of 96 years, arriving without warning in Little Figgy, with blood streaming down his face above his right eye, and his hands profusely bleeding, wearing white clothing, comprising of upper and lower garments, with one open sandal, and on top of his man bun grey hair, a blue and white yarmulke adorned his head. He has eyes for Violet White-Walsh, the owner-chef of Little Figgy's Mudders Restaurant, the only upscale vegetarian vegan restaurant in the village. It is he who has stretched out his hand to Jakob, who according to Dr Piddy Adfat, is suffering from SAD, Social Anxiety Disorder.

During the ensuing days, it was Yitzhak who brought Jakob and Junia, the widow Murphy, together. All three of them agreed to meet covertly at a location known as the Rock located behind the Gates of Heaven Help Us, facing on one side DUFF's Playing Field and on the other a plot of land where the community co-op store, Tea & Teeth grew organic produce and ran various workshops for their members.

I would be surprised if you, the reader, didn't question me how I knew Junia, the widow Murphy might be able to reveal aspects of Jakob's character and psychological makeup. Simply put, I will respond in this way. To quote Nicolaus Copernicus, "To know that we know what we know, and to know that we do not know what we do not know, that is true knowledge".

When Love Conquers All

If there's nothing more that connects a reader to a story it is a tale of love, romance, and intrigue, I know not what! And that is what is about to happen. I will call it, *"The romantic journey between Nurse Tryphena of the Little Figgy Medical Centre and Rodney Parsons, the co-manager of Tea & Teeth, Little Figgy's Co-op Grocery Store."*

As you might recollect, Nurse Tryphena suffers from Body Dysmorphic Disorder (BDD). She spends an inordinate amount of time worrying about imperfections in her appearance. Her dream to become a dance trapeze artiste came to an abrupt end when Dr Piddy Adfat suggested an excessive period hanging upside down, as you know, many dance trapeze artiste do, could result in an increase in blood pressure to her eyes that may damage them.

Nurse Tryphena was devastated. However, her friend Rodney Parsons, continued to give her the emotional support befitting of someone in his position. Their marriage followed. Our Father Murphy officiated and our Yitzhak, as expected of him, gave a warm toast to the bride and groom.

The couple took up residence in a lovely two-bedroom house, painted in the colours of white, blue, red, and gold, located on the west side of the Little Figgy Pond just behind the Little Figgy Co-op Grocery Store and Jötunn and Lisa White's bakery and butcher store.

Surrounding their house, the newly married couple planted a profusion of Sarracenia purpurea L. You would, I'm sure, obviously know it as the insect-eating pitcher plant, a plant not at all appreciated by the local arachnids.

Nurse Tryphena and Rodney were inseparable. So it seemed! However, a few months into their marriage and on the insistence of his wife, Rodney visited Dr Piddy Adfat. She diagnosed Rodney with a condition called philematophobia, an extreme fear of kissing.

Dr Piddy Adfat's diagnosis took on a whole new

meaning for the couple. Their marriage vows were in disarray, Rodney, before his marriage, was a sort of quiet chap who took his role in life very seriously in growing organic fruits and vegetables, running workshop classes, and with his friend, the entomologist Wayne White, the Athletic Turf Manager of the Little Figgy's DUFF Playing Field, he would organize village walks within the forest discussing the ability of various insects to track odours to their sources. He had, if I can put it to you, the makings of becoming one of Little Figgy's accomplished human beings.

But now? He had become very distant. He had almost given up helping his twin brother Terry with running the Tea & Teeth Co-op Store, preferring to take solitary walks in the forest, while observing the birdish antics of the Common Treecreeper, the Eurasian Griffon, and on some days, even the Little Ringed Plover.

And what of Nurse Tryphena? As recommended by Dr Piddy Adfat, based on her health inhibiting her work performance, she took time off from the Little Figgy Medical Centre. Tryphena's twin sister, Nurse Tryphosa, being as they say of sound mind, was quite capable of standing in for her.

Tryphena, in the meantime, returned to her dad's Jigs Diner, helping out the best she could, serving the customers but always talking about her lost opportunity of becoming a dance trapeze artiste.

Today, as you enter the Diner, if you glance towards the far end, by the window, overlooking The Gates of Heaven Help Us, you will see hanging on the wall, a short pre-taped horizontal bar dangling from two ropes, and a one-piece leotard handmade costume in stretched velvet, crystal-embellished and hand-painted beautifully throughout.

Ai-ai-ai! It is what it is!

Little Figgy's Fahey-Fizzard Twins and How to Regain Friendship

The Jigs Diner, on Monday and Friday, between the morning hours of seven-thirty and nine-thirty, also doubles up as a regular meeting place for Little Figgy's senior seniors. It is a club, of sorts, called FIGS, comprising of some seven to nine men and two women who embrace their passion for the arts such as dance, drama, and music.

If you're wondering, I must add for clarity, none of the group would ever consider attending the Jigs Diner's Sunday morning breakfasts.

They all have their place outside, under two and one-half large patio umbrellas, on the corner of the property, among the wrought iron coffee tables and chairs, all of which are enclosed with a delightful selection of black wooden flower boxes facing the Little Figgy Pond that are filled with red hydrangeas, while the little birds of the morning wait patiently for any morsels of food being dropped on the floor.

It is an interesting sight to observe. Most of the time the characters, while drinking their fresh mint tea, just look at each other, or simply acknowledge a passer-by out for a morning stroll with the dog.

If there is a thought of expressing a view, it usually commences and immediately ends with a, "do you remember when...?" which constitutes a response by a grunt or nod of the head and always the raising of the eyebrows.

But, I have to tell you, all of that changed quite recently with the addition of our Yitzhak who, without knowing the ground rules, sat on a chair in an area that had been reserved for countless years by Little Figgy's Fahey-Fizzard twins, Fanny and Flora. Yitzhak's error caused quite a disturbance as those sitting around him gave him a fair warning of what would be in store for him. Nevertheless, Yitzhak being a friendly, likeable fellow merely poo-pooed all of the warnings and waited for the first opportunity to meet Fanny and Flora.

In the meantime, dear reader, you must have perceived by now, as I have, that there are several twins living in Little Figgy.

However, in the case of the Fahey-Fizzard twins, their story is so fascinating it is one that I will now share with you.

Fanny and Flora are unique, as it were – who isn't unique in Little Figgy? The family name, Fahey-Fizzard is their theatrical name and one they now prefer to use full-time. It was introduced we are told, by their maternal grandmother's thespian family who wanted to be distinct from all the other Little Figgy names such as the Parsons, White, Walsh, Murphy, and Brown families. In that, they succeeded!

They are one of the very few, if not the only Little Figgy family who, through historical documents, can trace their lineage back to the founding fathers and mothers who landed by chance on the Mediterranean sands in an area in France now known as the village of Salin-de-Giraud located 40km west of the city of Arles in the Provence region in southern France. Arles, as I'm sure you remember, is renowned for inspiring many of the paintings of Van Gogh.

Sadly, Fanny and Flora are the last of their dynasty. Throughout their lives, they preferred their roles of being chameleon thespians. Their deep passion for acting exceeded their preference for family life. Neither of them married.

At a young age, their parents obliged them with ancient stories about the indigenous people who traditionally inhabited Newfoundland and Labrador. Tales of the Beothuk, Innu, and Inuit became bedtime stories. The stories, of which we have no reason to dispute, fascinated the girls and over the years every Sunday afternoon at the Little Figgy Cultural Centre to a packed house they would perform as heroines of a bygone age.

And now, at the age of 97 years, suffering from acute spectrophobia, they have had to retire from the theatre world, preferring these days to take their place every Monday and Friday, between the morning hours of seven-thirty and nine-thirty, at the Jigs Diner, sipping on their mint tea amongst their friends quietly acknowledging with a smile and a twinkle in their eyes anyone passing by who recognises them. Very few do!

And then came Yitzhak!

Their meeting, to say the least, had all the makings of an extraordinary theatrical stage event, about which I will now tell you. I will set the backstory.

Yitzhak, is the stranger, with a multi-character

background, with personality changes that would make the average shapeshifter cringe with jealousy. He sits on the patio of the Diner, in all innocence, waiting patiently for Fanny and Flora to arrive. He is surrounded by a group of nine senior-seniors all impatient for the start of Act One.

Dear reader, I have never seen nine men of a certain age affected by all that they believed would happen. There they all were, ignoring the present, each sipping on their second cup of fresh mint tea, saying nothing to each other, waiting, eagerly waiting for the opportunity to observe the first act of the performance.

Curtain up! Fade in!

Fanny and Flora appear slowly from upstage stage right, walking, arm-in-arm, downstage. As they come into view, Yitzhak rises from his patio chair. His left hand, while holding the last remnants of his second cup of fresh mint tea, is shaking. With tears in both of his eyes, he puts down his tea on the table, raises both hands high in the air, and says out loudly to all those around him, "As my guru, Paramahansa Yogananda has said, learn to be calm and you will always be happy. Am I right, tell me I'm right?"

As the audience of nine men and now enhanced with a circle of passing villagers, all looking on in utter confusion, Fanny and Flora step forward. Flora, in her left hand, is carrying a priceless zamphona, a medieval six-string instrument, while her right hand offers Yitzhak an off-white facial tissue.

As it's been said before now, no theatre director could have accomplished such a visual effect as what was witnessed by all those watching the event. Nor could a playwright produce such emotional words that Yitzhak expressed.

I continue.

"Toltse? Henda? Is it you?"

"Yes, Yitzhak, it is us. But here, in Little Figgy, we now call ourselves by our stage names, Fanny and Flora. We are the Fahey-Fizzard twins!"

Fade out!

Dear reader, I pause here, for I am beginning to sense your downright confusion as to what is happening.

Yitzhak, AKA., der anderer rebbe, the self-proclaimed Jewish guru named Gurdayal the Compassionate, had at one time, many years ago, in the village of Little Pletzl-on-the-Zump, been Fanny's lover!

Fanny and Flora, or for the sake of simplicity, I

will call them Toltse and Henda, grew up in Little Figgy, but then, when their parents separated they moved for some years to Little Pletzl where they listed to stories of how, in the old country, their father's family were involved in raising sheep.

The stories fascinated the girls, and as they grew up they vowed to become sheep shearers. Their story now becomes more than interesting.

As it's been written, one early spring sunny afternoon, while on their walk among Little Pletzl's bushes and shrubs, they came across a small flock of lost Préalpes-du-Sud sheep wandering aimlessly in front of them. Without any consequences of the laws governing the stealing of sheep, they somehow steered the sheep and . . .

The girls fled and somehow, I know not how, ended up in Little Figgy-on-the-Duff.

I have to admit, even though I have Welsh Wales roots in me, I know nothing about sheep, nor can I distinguish the difference between a Little Pletzl Préalpes-du-Sud from an Arles Merinos breed, which I believe was an integral part of the original story.

What I can say to you now, with utter conviction, I am sure Toltse and her sister Henda, if they had stayed in Little Pletzl, would have had a good chance of becoming Golden Shears World Sheep Shearing and Wool Handling Champions. That was their commitment to raising sheep. But all this happened so long ago.

Now we will return today, to Little Figgy and to Yitzhak, Fanny, and Flora.

Fade to black.

As one would expect, all the Figgy people surrounding them, by now there was quite a crowd, had no idea what they were talking about, partly because half the time they were speaking in Frantsoydish, the language from the old country spoken in Little Pletzl, and the other half, Yitzhak, Fanny, and Flora were either laughing, crying or holding each other's hands.

And for the nine Figgy men, of a certain age, who had waited patiently drinking their second cup of mint tea, in anticipation of watching a right squabble, were so gobsmacked by the event taking place, they all got up en masse and headed for the Little Figgy Cultural Centre. They signed up to take a morning course, given by our Father Murphy, called, *'How to Become an Expert in Piddling.'*

As for Fanny and Flora, Yitzhak escorted them

back to his temporary quarters in the Little Figgy Medical Centre, where he made them a home-made roasted eggplant and pickle beet sandwich, as they all shared nostalgic memories of bygone times while Jakob listened.

And, in concluding this charming chapter about love and friendship, I will refer you to what Yitzhak said to Jakob. "Jakob, just remember what Euripides, the great dramatist said. 'One loyal friend is worth ten thousand relatives.'"

The Little Figgy Fysshynge wyth an Angle day

If there is one day in the year that is celebrated more than any other in Little Figgy, it is without doubt, the festival of the 'Little Figgy Fysshynge wyth an Angle day', fêted since 1495, every year on June 29. To us simple ordinary folks you might know it as International Fisherman's Day.

It was earlier this year that Mayor Sadie Parsons announced the appointment of Zebedee and his wife Karen Parsons of Burbots Fish and Chip Shop as her choice to be Little Figgy's joint honorary chairs of the 'Little Figgy Fysshynge wyth an Angle day.'

"I believe we have found and appointed exactly

who we need to lead our 'Fysshynge wyth an Angle day'," she proudly announced as loudly as possible while eating her fish cakes, made with potatoes, burbot, onions, and herbs, served with baked beans, and a side order of boiled eggs, to all those who would listen to her at the regular Sunday morning breakfast at Jigs Diner,

I can say to you, that the Mayor's decision was not unexpected, but it did cause other questions to be raised by some members of her cabinet at their Monday lunch at Mudders Restaurant before Little Figgy's council meeting.

Present were Mayor Sadie Parsons, Deputy Mayor Lisa Walsh, the Executive Committee members led by our Father John Murphy, and Zebedee Parsons, Enosh Walsh-White, Business Manager Annie White-Brown, and Dr Piddy Adfat.

Enosh Walsh-White initiated the conversation.

"Yes, I saw it all," announced Enosh Walsh-White. "This morning, at the Jigs Diner, on the patio, in front of everyone. All three of them, hugging and crying, talking in some sort of foreign language."

"Wad-a-Pity," responded Dr Piddy Adfat. "Baba, my husband, has some serious reservations about, you know, the stranger."

"Yes, I know what you mean, some of my customers think Karen and I should ask him to be on our Fysshynge wyth an Angle day committee," piped in Zebedee Parsons. "He admits he knows nothing about angling, let alone what a burbot is. And as far as the Little Figgy Pond, he spends hours at the edge reflectively thinking about something or other."

"Perhaps he thinks he can walk on water," added Annie White-Brown, with a quiet smirk on her face."

"Tundering Jaysus! Enough!" screamed our Father Murphy, as he stood up, bright red with rage, banging his fist down on the table. "Have you all lost your minds?

"O mi Iesu, dimitte nobis debita nostra, salva nos ab igne inferni, perduc in caelum omnes animas, praesertim eas, quae misericordiae tuae maxime indigent."

And with those words reflecting his views on hate and mercy, the lunch erupted into chaos with our Father Murphy storming out, while the others wondered what just had happened.

Our Father Murphy took the long way back to his beloved church, The Gates of Heaven Help Us. Past the Little Figgy Medical Centre with its muster of peacocks and peahens pecking at the ground. Past the Tea & Teeth Co-op Grocery Store. Past White's Bakery. Past the Little Figgy Pub, after stopping for a quick pint of Little Figgy beer. Past Gabriel White's police constabulary, while giving a short pat to Goobies, the dog. Past the Jigs Diner, not stopping to acknowledge the many 'whaddya ats!' and finally when arriving at his church he paused, looked up above the church's entrance at the old plaque with the words, 'Quaerite primum regnum dei', (*See ye first the kingdom of God),* and with tears in his eyes said, "Yitzhak, whoever you are, It is time for you to return to your home."

I return now to the festival of the 'Little Figgy Fysshynge wyth an Angle day'.

The morning had started rather cloudy, but by mid-morning, the sun was in full flair. The Little Figgy Pond was surrounded by a perfusion of multi-colored bunting flags in celebration of the event. Each fabric flag had been made at the Little Figgy Community Centre under the patronage of the Little Figgy Flag Committee in support and coordinate efforts to enhance good neighbourly relations during appropriate holidays and events.

The chair of the committee, Margaret Brown, the Executive Director of the Little Figgy Cultural

Centre, is an outstanding vexillographer. Handed down from generation to generation, today there isn't anyone in the village who knows more about how to design a bunting flag than our Margaret. For generations, her family has been regarded as the village vexillologists.

I have to admit, if at all possible, I might want to give serious consideration in nominating Margaret Brown to be the next president of The International Fabric Bunting Federation of Vexillological Associations.

Our Margaret, after serious reflection, put together a worthy eclectic, and dynamic group of Little Figgy Flag Committee members including, Rosie White-Walsh the daughter of Violet White-Walsh of Mudders Restaurant, Wayne Brown-White, the village's Entomologist, Olivia Brown the daughter of William Brown the publican of Chummy's Pub, and Jötunn White the baker, butcher, and veterinary pathologist.

On hand, during the first day of the Little Figgy Flag Committee member's meeting, our Father John Murphy, ever-present at all these propitious occasions, was asked to say a prayer.

"For all those present today, I ask you to bless this meeting. Provide us with your support…" He paused and raised his eyes upward. "Prepare us all for those we will encounter afterward. Ready us to make every moment count. Amen."

Ah yes! Dear reader, the circumstances on what we know of our Father Murphy's present condition, would lead us to presume he is going through some difficult personal issues relating to his religious convictions. This leads me to tell you of what little I know, or for that matter, what anyone knows, about our Father John Murphy.

John Murphy was welcomed into the church at the young age of 13 years by Father Mathew White-Parsons. John was regarded as a superb chorister as well as being an avid reader. His parents had hopes of him going into managing Little Figgy forested and woodland areas, just like his dad. But John was devoted to the church's ways. "I have a calling inside me," he would say to his parents. Over time, he ferociously read many of the philosophy and theology books offered to him by Father Mathew. John Murphy became lost in omphaloskepsis. His friends deserted him as he became more entrenched in church affairs.

"John, there is more to Little Figgy's life than the Gates of Heaven Help Us," his girlfriend at the time, now known as Mayor Sadie Parsons, would say to him. But John was unyielding.

And in time, it came to pass…Father Mathew ordained John Murphy into the priesthood. A few weeks later, Father Mathew voluntarily requested he be removed from the clerical state for a grave and personal reason, of which we have no further knowledge.

Sadly, he died suddenly on June 29, while our Father John was at his side, on the patio of the Jigs Diner, on the actual day of the 'Little Figgy Fysshynge wyth an Angle day', after swallowing an entire touton, a hard doughy, fried bread dough ball served with molasses, which he had dipped into his second cup of fresh mint tea.

It was left to a shaken, nervous, and youngish our Father John Murphy to conduct the Requiem Mass for his mentor, Father Mathew White-Parsons.

It is said, by those who know our Father John from the old days that he never recovered from the event, nor did a touton, from that time onward, ever touch his lips.

O Junia, Where Art Thou?

Junia, the widow Murphy, in case I have to remind you, is the Little Figgy Gates of Heaven Help Us church carillonneur, and member of the Passalorynchite Christian sect, who many years ago, much to the relief and wishes of her neighbours, had taken a vow of perpetual silence. She is also what we today perhaps would identify, in the traditional biblical sense, as a modern-day apostle elder in the apostolic movement.

As previously said, she is hospitable, sensitive and a kindly perspicacious character, slim as a rake, standing at the best of times, a petite 55 cm tall, widowed for many years, and is enjoying her life to the extreme, although many of Little Figgy's villagers would question that fact! But, what do they know? On the whole, she comes across as a shy and quiet person. She tends to notice things other people miss. All I would prefer to add to that is the quote, 'Never judge a book by its cover,' which, in my opinion, is entirely a picture-perfect representation of her.

To those of you who may be wondering what happened to the late Mr. Junia? Well, what I understand is one Friday night, after drinking his customarily four pints of beer at the Chummy's Pub, upon exiting, and in a fit of jubilation, staggered in pitch-darkness towards the deep end of the Little Figgy Pond, slipped, fell into the water, and simply drowned.

Junia, now the window Murphy, after several sessions with Dr Piddy Adfat, expressed a wish to learn as much as possible about becoming a social therapist, a profession much needed in Little Figgy. Junia enthusiastically threw herself into years of intense study with Dr Piddy Adfat, and after a period of time, she was given the accreditation of being a licensed mental health counsellor.

Her very first client? Jakob, the son of Mayor Sadie Parsons and Mr. Jack Parsons. Jakob, as you remember from an earlier chapter, suffers from a form of Social Anxiety Disorder.

And now, I will continue from where an earlier chapter left off.

It was Yitzhak who brought Jakob and Junia, the widow Murphy, together. All three of them agreed to meet covertly at a location known as the Rock located behind the Gates of Heaven Help Us, facing on one side DUFF's Playing Field and on the other a plot of land where the community co-op store, Tea & Teeth grew organic produce and ran various workshops for their paid members.

Waiting for them, sitting on the Rock reading a book was a man not unlike the image of our Yitzhak, by the name of Raphael. Junia introduced him as her friend. What struck me was his remarkable likeness to that of Yitzhak. The same man bun hairstyle, his stature, similar white clothing, and a pair of brown sandals.

Raphael was accompanied by a Bichon Frise sitting quietly on his lap.

"Yitzhak. This is my friend Raphael. He is Little Figgy's spiritual healer and protector. He is also my invisible teacher. He wanted to meet you."

Raphael arose from the Rock, his Bichon Frise cupped in his left hand. As a gesture of friendship, he extended his right hand towards Yitzhak and smiled at him.

"Shalom, Yitzhak, I am here to help you on your journey home. Your friends are waiting for you just beyond the forest edge, over there." He pointed to a distant group of trees and turned towards Jakob who had, by image, changed from a young shy man to that of an imposing figure.

"Yitzhak, my friend Jakob will guide you on your journey. Listen to advice and accept instruction, that you may gain wisdom in the future."

Jakob gently put his hand on Yitzhak's shoulder. "They are all waiting for you, Yitzhak. Your friends are so anxious to see you again. Your friends from Little Pletzl. Dr Christin Wójcik, twin nurses Frayda and Pesha, Rabbi Dudel ben Shalom, your companion Shprintza, Feyervaser from Shenken the Distillery, and also many more from Little Comely. Dr Moshe Jacobs, twin nurses Felicity and Penelope, Hairy Thomas, Owain Jones the butcher, and Wellesley Llewellyn from the Duke of Wellington Pub."

Dear reader, I'm sorry you were unable to be present. If you had been you would have seen the utter bewilderment on Yitzhak's face as he took one step backward in shock, slipped on a patch of wet earth, and ended up hitting his head, above his right eye, on a batch of stones.

"Junia, Jakob, Raphael. I'm confused. I don't understand what is happening, I intended to follow the travels of Gershon ben Eliezer ha-Levi and write an account of my journey, crossing the impossible Sambation River, beyond which, as it has been told, the Ten Lost Tribes of Israel were banished by the Assyrian king Shalmaneser V. And now?"

Raphael stepped forward. "Yitzhak, a great novelist and short story writer I believe once said, Confusion is a word we have invented for an order which is not understood."

Raphael helped Yitzhak get up. "Yes, we understand your confusion. Come, let me stop the bleeding above your right eye."

Whoever walks with the wise becomes wise

Walking unhurriedly toward the forest, Yitzhak and Jakob stopped, surprised at the hullabaloo all the Little Figgy villagers were making who had come out to watch their parting. Only Yitzhak turned to face them, while Jakob walked on ahead.

There was Jim still with his STOP sign held high above him waving goodbye. Chief Constable Gabriel White was making his customary grunting noises, while his dog, Goobies sat quietly observing those around him. The twin nurses Tryphosa and Tryphena Brown waved to Yitzhak who noted Tryphena had donned for the occasion her dance trapeze artiste costume.

Delbert Brown sang "We bid adieu unto our friend", while Mrs Blanche White handed out to everyone helpings of her partridgeberry cake.

Mrs Violet White-Walsh of Mudders Restaurant ran up to Yitzhak and presented him with four of her baked mug cakes and a flask of honey.

William Brown of Chummy's Pub, never to miss a special happening, arrived in time to present Yitzhak with four bottles of Little Figgy Beer. He was followed by Luke Brown of Jigs Diner with a basket containing four boiled eggs, a block of cheese, and a loaf of sourdough bread.

Not everyone turned out. Missing were Mayor Sadie Parsons and her husband Jack. Missing were Dr Piddy Adfat, her husband Baba Younus, and their peacocks and peahens. Missing were Zebedee Parsons and Little Figgy's lawyer, Enosh White-Walsh.

Yitzhak gestured to the crowd in a manner, not unlike he had done some months ago on leaving Little Pletzl-on-the-Zump. Walking slowly towards the forest, he stopped, turned, and looked back at all the curiosity seekers who had come to watch his farewell.

Yitzhak waved, said his goodbyes to all the Little Figgys, and quickly caught up with Jakob as the villagers' presence faded behind them into the background.

Neither of them spoke.

Waiting for them at the forest edge hidden amongst the bushes and trees were our Father John Murphy and Jötunn White the baker, butcher, and veterinary pathologist. Jötunn White, with a smile, approached Yitzhak.

"Yes, Yitzhak. Do you remember, when you arrived in Little Figgy, I whispered the words to you that only you heard? I said, 'but you can call me Joo for short!' But now, dear friend, you can call me by my actual name, Joseph."

Our Father John Murphy stepped forward. "And I aim to follow you, Yitzhak, whoever you are, I believe in you and . . ."

Jakob held up his hands and turned to Yitzhak.

"It is decision time for you, Yitzhak. Tell us. Do we all turn left to meet your friends from Little Comely-on-the-Marsh and from Little Pletzl-on-the-Zump who are waiting in anticipation for your arrival? Or do we all turn right to follow, as you have told us, the travels of Gershon ben Eliezer ha-Levi so that you may write an account of your journey, crossing the impossible Sambation River, beyond which, as it has been told, the Ten Lost Tribes of Israel were banished by the Assyrian king Shalmaneser V?

"Yitzhak, what is it to be?"

ABOUT THE AUTHOR

Alan L. Simons is an author, writer, and social & allyship advocate. He was born and educated in London, England, where he worked for various newspapers before immigrating to Canada. As a diplomat, he served as the Honorary Consul of the Republic of Rwanda to Canada, in the post-genocide era. He lectures and writes on issues relating to religion in politics, antisemitism, intolerance, hate, Islamofascism, conflict, and terrorism. The Village of Little Figgy-on-the-Duff is his seventh published book the third in the Village trilogy.

Other Books by Alan L. Simons

EIGHTEEN MONTHS-A LOVE STORY INTERRUPTED

A story of a human relationship that testifies to the strength and will of both the terminally ill patient and her partner as he comes to accept her illness and the short period of time they will spend together.

THE VILLAGE OF LITTLE COMELY-ON-THE-MARSH

This hilarious and satirical story weaves around the lives of an eccentric Welsh community living in a small village somewhere in southern of France exclusively in their own sheltered world.

THE VILLAGE OF LITTLE PLETZL-ON-THE-ZUMP

The Village of Little Pletzl-on-the-Zump is the sequel to the book *The Village of Little Comely-on-the-Marsh*. Pletzl, the story, weaves around the lives of a bizarre Yiddish-speaking community of 613 people living for hundreds of years in a small village somewhere in southern France. They speak a distinctive Yiddish dialect called Frantsoydish.

THE CHILDREN OF THE FOREST

Written for both grown-ups and older children. Loosely based on a story by Rabbi Nahman of Bratslav. A folktale in the European tradition. Kabbalistic, Mystical, Esoteric, Freygish. An account of two Polish Jewish children from pre-teens to adulthood, together with five mystical characters and Klezmer musicians.

THE INCREDIBLE ADVENTURES OF CAPTAIN MACDUDDYFUNK IN CUGGERMUGGERLAND

The children of Canada's Minister of Missing Islands, are magically transported to the mysterious island of Cuggermuggerland where they meet the Quidnuncs, who love to hug, and the Shilpits, who always scream and shout at each other.

SWEATY CATS AND BABY PIGEONS

A series of short stories written for the inquiring mind of a young child, in which grandparents can interact and stimulate communication between the generations.

https://alanlsimons.wordpress.com

figgyontheduff@proton.me

alsimons@proton.me

www.ingramcontent.com/pod-product-compliance
Lightning Source LLC
Chambersburg PA
CBHW051839170626
46807CB00003B/1253